"THE INDISCREET LETTER"
AND "LITTLE EVE EDGARTON"

"THE INDISCREET LETTER" AND "LITTLE EVE EDGARTON"

ELEANOR HALLOWELL ABBOTT

WILDSIDE PRESS

THE INDISCREET LETTER

Published by Wildside Press, LLC
www.wildsidepress.com

CONTENTS

THE INDISCREET LETTER

The Railroad Journey was very long and slow. The Traveling Salesman was rather short and quick. And the Young Electrician who lolled across the car aisle was neither one length nor another, but most inordinately flexible, like a suit of chain armor.

More than being short and quick, the Traveling Salesman was distinctly fat and unmistakably dressy in an ostentatiously new and pure-looking buff-colored suit, and across the top of the shiny black sample-case that spanned his knees he sorted and re-sorted with infinite earnestness a large and varied consignment of "Ladies' Pink and Blue Ribbed Undervests." Surely no other man in the whole southward-bound Canadian train could have been at once so ingenuous and so nonchalant.

There was nothing dressy, however, about the Young Electrician. From his huge cowhide boots to the lead smouch that ran from his rough, square chin to the very edge of his astonishingly blond curls, he was one delicious mess of toil and old clothes and smiling, blue-eyed indifference. And every time that he shrugged his shoulders or crossed his knees he jingled and jangled incongruously among his coil-boxes and insulators, like some splendid young Viking of old, half blacked up for a modern minstrel show.

More than being absurdly blond and absurdly messy, the Young Electrician had one of those extraordinarily sweet, extraordinarily vital, strangely mysterious, utterly unexplainable masculine faces that fill your senses with an odd, impersonal disquietude, an itching unrest, like the hazy, teasing reminder of some previous existence in a prehistoric cave, or, more tormenting still, with the tingling, psychic prophecy of some amazing emotional experience yet to come. The sort of face, in fact, that almost inevitably flares up into a woman's startled vision at the one crucial moment in her life when she is not supposed to be considering alien features.

Out from the servient shoulders of some smooth-tongued Waiter it stares, into the scared dilating pupils of the White Satin Bride with her pledged hand clutching her Bridegroom's sleeve. Up from the gravelly, pick-and-shovel labor of the new-made grave it lifts its weirdly magnetic eyes to the Widow's tears. Down from some petted Princeling's silver-trimmed saddle horse it smiles its electrifying, wistful smile into the Peasant's sodden weariness. Across the slender white rail of an always *outgoing* steamer it stings back into your gray, landlocked consciousness like the tang of a scarlet spray. And the secret of the face, of course, is "Lure"; but to save your soul you could not decide in any specific case whether the lure is the lure of personality, or the lure of physiognomy — a mere accidental, coincidental, haphazard harmony of forehead and cheekbone and twittering facial muscles.

Something, indeed, in the peculiar set of the Young Electrician's jaw warned you quite definitely that if you should ever even so much as hint the small, sentimental word "lure" to him he would most certainly "swat" you on first impulse for a maniac, and on second impulse for a liar — smiling at you all the while in the strange little wrinkly tissue round his eyes.

The voice of the Railroad Journey was a dull, vague, conglomerate, cinder-scented babble of grinding wheels and shuddering window frames; but the voices of the Traveling Salesman and the Young Electrician were shrill, gruff, poignant, inert, eternally variant, after the manner of human voices which are discussing the affairs of the universe.

"Every man," affirmed the Traveling Salesman sententiously — "every man has written one indiscreet letter during his lifetime!"

"Only one?" scoffed the Young Electrician with startling distinctness above even the loudest roar and rumble of the train.

With a rather faint, rather gaspy chuckle of amusement the Youngish Girl in the seat just behind the Traveling Salesman reached forward then and touched him very gently on the shoulder.

"Oh, please, may I listen?" she asked quite frankly.

With a smile as benevolent as it was surprised, the Traveling Salesman turned halfway around in his seat and eyed her quizzically across the gold rim of his spectacles.

"Why, sure you can listen!" he said.

The Traveling Salesman was no fool. People as well as lisle thread were a specialty of his. Even in his very first smiling estimate of the Youngish Girl's face, neither vivid blond hair nor luxuriantly ornate furs misled him for an instant. Just as a Preacher's high waistcoat passes him, like an official badge of dignity and honor, into any conceivable kind of a situation, so also does a woman's high forehead usher her with delicious impunity into many conversational experiences that would hardly be wise for her lower-browed sister.

With an extra touch of manners the Salesman took off his neat brown derby hat and placed it carefully on the vacant seat in front of him. Then, shifting his sample-case adroitly to suit his new twisted position, he began to stick cruel little prickly price marks through alternate meshes of pink and blue lisle.

"Why, sure you can listen!" he repeated benignly. "Traveling alone's awful stupid, ain't it? I reckon you were glad when the busted heating apparatus in the sleeper gave you a chance to come in here and size up a few new faces. Sure you can listen! Though, bless your heart, we weren't talking about anything so very specially interesting," he explained conscientiously. "You see, I was merely arguing with my young friend here that if a woman really loves you, she'll follow you through any kind of blame or disgrace — follow you anywheres, I said — anywheres!"

"Not anywheres," protested the Young Electrician with a grin. "'Not up a telegraph pole!'" he requoted sheepishly.

"Y-e-s — I heard that," acknowledged the Youngish Girl with blithe shamelessness.

"Follow you 'anywheres,' was what I said," persisted the Traveling Salesman almost irritably. "Follow you 'anywheres'! Run! Walk! Crawl on her hands and knees if it's really necessary. And yet —" Like a shaggy brown line drawn across the bottom of a column of figures, his eyebrows narrowed to their final calculation. "And yet —" he estimated cautiously, "and yet — there's times when I ain't so almighty sure that her following you is any more specially flattering to you than if you was a burglar. She don't follow you so much, I reckon, because you *are* her love as because you've *got* her love. God knows it ain't just you, yourself, she's afraid of losing. It's what she's already invested in you that's worrying her! All her pinky-posy, cunning kid-dreams about loving and marrying, maybe; and the pretty much grown-up winter she fought out the whisky question with you, perhaps; and the summer you had the typhoid, likelier than not; and the spring the youngster was born — oh, sure, the spring the youngster was born! Gee! If by swallowing just one more yarn you tell her, she can only keep on holding down all the old yarns you ever told her — if, by forgiving you just one more forgive-you, she can only hang on, as it were, to the original worthwhileness of the whole darned business — if by —"

"Oh, that's what you meant by the 'whole darned business,' was it?" cried the Youngish Girl suddenly, edging away out to the front of her seat. Along the curve of her cheeks an almost mischievous smile began to quicken. "Oh, yes! I heard that, too!" she confessed cheerfully. "But what was the beginning of it all? The very beginning? What was the first thing you said? What started you talking about it? Oh, please, excuse me for hearing anything at all," she finished abruptly; "but I've been traveling alone now for five dreadful days, all the way down from British Columbia, and — if — you — will — persist — in — saying interesting things — in trains — you must take the consequences!"

There was no possible tinge of patronage or condescension in her voice, but rather, instead, a bumpy, naive sort of friendliness, as lonesome Royalty sliding temporarily down from its throne might reasonably contend with each bump, "A King may look at a cat! He may! He may!"

Along the edge of the Young Electrician's cheekbones the red began to flush furiously. He seemed to have a funny little way of blushing just before he spoke, and the physical mannerism gave an absurdly italicized sort of emphasis to even the most trivial thing that he said.

"I guess you'll have to go ahead and tell her about 'Rosie,'" he suggested grinningly to the Traveling Salesman.

"Yes! Oh, do tell me about 'Rosie,'" begged the Youngish Girl with whimsical eagerness. "Who in creation was 'Rosie'?" she persisted laughingly. "I've been utterly mad about 'Rosie' for the last half-hour!"

"Why, 'Rosie' is nobody at all — probably," said the Traveling Salesman a trifle wryly.

"Oh, pshaw!" flushed the Young Electrician, crinkling up all the little smile-tissue around his blue eyes. "Oh, pshaw! Go ahead and tell her about 'Rosie.'"

"Why, I tell you it wasn't anything so specially interesting," protested the Traveling Salesman diffidently. "We simply got jollying a bit in the first place about the amount of perfectly senseless, no-account truck that'll collect in a fellow's pockets; and then some sort of a scorched piece of paper he had, or something, got him telling me about a nasty, sizzling close call he had today with a live wire; and then I got telling him here about a friend of mine — and a mighty good fellow, too — who dropped dead on the street one day last summer with an unaddressed, typewritten letter in his pocket that began 'Dearest Little Rosie,' called her a 'Honey' and a 'Dolly Girl' and a 'Pink-Fingered Precious,' made a rather foolish dinner appointment for Thursday in New Haven, and was signed — in the Lord's own time — at the end of four pages, 'Yours forever, and then some. tom.' — Now the wife of the deceased was named — Martha."

Quite against all intention, the Youngish Girl's laughter rippled out explosively and caught up the latent amusement in the Young Electrician's face. Then, just as unexpectedly, she wilted back a little into her seat.

"I don't call that an 'indiscreet letter'!" she protested almost resentfully. "You might call it a knavish letter. Or a foolish letter. Because either a knave or a fool surely wrote it! But 'indiscreet'? U-m-m, No!"

"Well, for heaven's sake!" said the Traveling Salesman. "If — you — don't — call — that — an — indiscreet letter, what would you call one?"

"Yes, sure," gasped the Young Electrician, "what would you call one?" The way his lips mouthed the question gave an almost tragical purport to it.

"What would I call an 'indiscreet letter'?" mused the Youngish Girl slowly. "Why — why — I think I'd call an 'indiscreet letter' a letter that was pretty much — of a gamble perhaps, but a letter that was perfectly, absolutely legitimate for you to send, because it would be your own interests and your own life that you were gambling with, not the happiness of your wife or the honor of your husband. A letter, perhaps, that might be a trifle risky — but a letter, I mean, that is absolutely on the square!"

"But if it's absolutely 'on the square,'" protested the Traveling Salesman, worriedly, "then where in creation does the 'indiscreet' come in?"

The Youngish Girl's jaw dropped. "Why, the 'indiscreet' part comes in," she argued, "because you're not able to prove in advance, you know, that the stakes you're gambling for are absolutely 'on the square.' I don't know exactly how to express it, but it seems somehow as though only the very little things of Life are offered in open packages — that all the big things come sealed very tight. You can poke them a little and make a guess at the shape, and you can rattle them a little and make a guess at the size, but you can't ever open them and prove them — until the money is paid down and gone forever from your hands. But goodness me!" she cried, brightening perceptibly; "if you were to put an advertisement in the biggest newspaper in the biggest city in the world, saying: 'Every person who has ever written an indiscreet letter in his life is hereby invited to attend a mass-meeting' — and if people would really go — you'd see the most distinguished public gathering that you ever saw in your life! Bishops and Judges and Statesmen and Beautiful Society Women and Little Old White-Haired Mothers — everybody, in fact, who had ever had red blood enough at least once in his life to write down in cold black and white the one vital, quivering, questioning fact that happened to mean the most to him at that moment! But your 'Honey' and your 'Dolly Girl' and your 'Pink-Fingered Precious' nonsense! Why, it isn't real! Why, it doesn't even *make sense!*"

Again the Youngish Girl's laughter rang out in light, joyous, utterly superficial appreciation.

Even the serious Traveling Salesman succumbed at last.

"Oh, yes, I know it sounds comic," he acknowledged wryly. "Sounds like something out of a summer vaudeville show or a cheap Sunday supplement. But I don't suppose it sounded so specially blamed comic to the widow. I reckon she found it plenty-heap indiscreet enough to suit her. Oh, of course," he added hastily, "I know, and Martha knows that Thomkins wasn't at all that kind of a fool. And yet, after all — when you really settle right down to think about it, Thomkins' name was easily 'Tommy,' and Thursday sure enough was his day in New Haven, and it was a yard of red flannel that Martha had asked him to bring home to her — not the scarlet automobile veil that they found in his pocket. But 'Martha,' I says, of course, 'Martha, it sure does beat all how we fellows that travel round so much in cars and trains are always and forever picking up automobile veils — dozens of them, *dozens* — red, blue, pink, yellow — why, I wouldn't wonder if my wife had as many as thirty-four tucked away in her top bureau drawer!' — 'I wouldn't wonder,' says Martha, stooping lower and lower over Thomkins's blue cotton shirt that she's trying to cut down into rompers for the baby. 'And, Martha,' I says, 'that letter is just a joke. One of the boys sure put it up on him!' — 'Why, of course,' says Martha, with her mouth all puckered up crooked, as though a kid had stitched it on the machine. 'Why, of course! How dared you think —'"

Forking one bushy eyebrow, the Salesman turned and stared quizzically off into space.

"But all the samey, just between you and I," he continued judicially, "all the samey, I'll wager you anything you name that it ain't just death that's pulling Martha down day by day, and night by night, limper and lanker and clumsier-footed. Martha's got a sore thought. That's what ails her. And God help the crittur with a sore thought! God help anybody who's got any one single, solitary sick idea that keeps thinking on top of itself, over and over and over, boring into the past, bumping into the future, fussing, fretting, eternally festering. Gee! Compared to it, a tight shoe is easy slippers, and water dropping on your head is perfect peace! — Look close at Martha, I say. Every night when the blowsy old moon shines like courting time, every day when the butcher's bill comes home as big as a swollen elephant, when the crippled stepson tries to cut his throat again, when the youngest kid sneezes funny like his father — 'who was rosie? who was rosie?'"

"Well, who was Rosie?" persisted the Youngish Girl absent-mindedly.

"Why, Rosie was *nothing*!" snapped the Traveling Salesman; "nothing at all — probably." Altogether in spite of himself, his voice trailed off into a suspiciously minor key. "But all the same," he continued more vehemently, "all the same — it's just that little darned word 'probably' that's making all the mess and bother of it — because, as far as I can reckon, a woman can stand absolutely anything under God's heaven that she knows; but she just up and can't stand the littlest, teeniest, no-account sort of thing that she ain't sure of. Answers may kill 'em dead enough, but it's questions that eats 'em alive."

For a long, speculative moment the Salesman's gold-rimmed eyes went frowning off across the snow-covered landscape. Then he ripped off his glasses and fogged them very gently with his breath.

"Now — I — ain't — any — saint," mused the Traveling Salesman meditatively, "and I — ain't very much to look at, and being on the road ain't a business that would exactly enhance my valuation in the eyes of a lady who was actually looking out for some safe place to bank her affections; but I've never yet reckoned on running with any firm that didn't keep up to its advertising promises, and if a man's courtship ain't his own particular, personal advertising proposition — then I don't know anything about — *anything*! So if I should croak sudden any time in a railroad accident or a hotel fire or a scrap in a saloon, I ain't calculating on leaving my wife any very large amount of 'sore thoughts.' When a man wants his memory kept green, he don't mean — gangrene!

"Oh, of course," the Salesman continued more cheerfully, "a sudden croaking leaves any fellow's affairs at pretty raw ends — lots of queer, bitter-tasting things that would probably have been all right enough if they'd only had time to get ripe. Lots of things, I haven't a doubt, that would make my wife kind of mad, but nothing, I'm calculating, that she wouldn't understand. There'd be no questions coming in from the office, I mean, and no fresh talk from the road that she ain't got the information on hand to meet. Life insurance ain't by any means, in my mind, the only kind of protection that a man owes his widow. Provide for her Future — if you can! — That's my motto! — But a man's just a plain bum who don't provide for his own Past! She may have plenty of trouble in the years to come settling her own bills, but she ain't going to have any worry settling any of mine. I tell you, there'll be no ladies swelling round in crape at my funeral that my wife don't know by their first names!"

With a sudden startling guffaw the Traveling Salesman's mirth rang joyously out above the roar of the car.

"Tell me about your wife," said the Youngish Girl a little wistfully.

Around the Traveling Salesman's generous mouth the loud

laugh flickered down to a schoolboy's bashful grin.

"My wife?" he repeated. "Tell you about my wife? Why, there isn't much to tell. She's little. And young. And was a school-teacher. And I married her four years ago."

"And were happy — ever — after," mused the Youngish Girl teasingly.

"No!" contradicted the Traveling Salesman quite frankly. "No! We didn't find out how to be happy at all until the last three years!"

Again his laughter rang out through the car.

"Heavens! Look at me!" he said at last. "And then think of her! — Little, young, a school-teacher, too, and taking poetry to read on the train same as you or I would take a newspaper! Gee! What would you expect?" Again his mouth began to twitch a little. "And I thought it was her fault — 'most all of the first year," he confessed delightedly. "And then, all of a sudden," he continued eagerly, "all of a sudden, one day, more mischievous-spiteful than anything else, I says to her, 'We don't seem to be getting on so very well, do we?' And she shakes her head kind of slow. 'No, we don't!' she says. — 'Maybe you think I don't treat you quite right?' I quizzed, just a bit mad. — 'No, you don't! That is, not — exactly right,' she says, and came burrowing her head in my shoulder as cozy as could be. — 'Maybe you could show me how to treat you — righter,' I says, a little bit pleasanter. — 'I'm perfectly sure I could!' she says, half laughing and half crying. 'All you'll have to do,' she says, 'is just to watch me!' — 'Just watch what *you* do?' I said, bristling just a bit again. — 'No,' she says, all pretty and soft-like; 'all I want you to do is to watch what I *don't* do!'"

With slightly nervous fingers the Traveling Salesman reached up and tugged at his necktie as though his collar were choking him suddenly.

"So that's how I learned my table manners," he grinned, "and that's how I learned to quit cussing when I was mad round the house, and that's how I learned — oh, a great many things — and that's how I learned —" grinning broader and broader — "that's how I learned not to come home and talk all the time about the 'peach' whom I saw on the train or the street. My wife, you see, she's got a little scar on her face — it don't show any, but she's awful sensitive about it, and 'Johnny,' she says, 'don't you never notice that I don't ever rush home and tell *you* about the wonderful *slim* fellow who sat next to me at the theater, or the simply elegant *grammar* that I heard at the lecture? I can recognize a slim fellow when I see him, Johnny,' she says, 'and I like nice grammar as well as the next one, but praising 'em to you, dear, don't seem to me so awfully polite. Bragging about handsome women to a plain wife, Johnny,' she says, 'is just about as raw as bragging about rich men to a husband who's broke.'

"Oh, I tell you a fellow's a fool," mused the Traveling Salesman judicially, "a fellow's a fool when he marries who don't go to work deliberately to study and understand his wife. Women are awfully understandable if you only go at it right. Why, the only thing that riles them in the whole wide world is the fear that the man they've married ain't quite bright. Why, when I was first married I used to think that my wife was awful snippety about other women. But, Lord! when you point a girl out in the car and say, 'Well, ain't that girl got the most gorgeous head of hair you ever saw in your life?' and your wife says: 'Yes — Jordan is selling them puffs six for a dollar seventy-five this winter,' she ain't intending to be snippety at all. No! — It's only, I tell you, that it makes a woman feel just plain silly to think that her husband don't even know as much as she does. Why, Lord! she don't care how much you praise the grocer's daughter's style, or your stenographer's spelling, as long as you'll only show that you're *equally wise* to the fact that the grocer's daughter sure has a nasty temper, and that the stenographer's spelling is mighty near the best thing about her.

"Why, a man will go out and pay every cent he's got for a good hunting dog — and then snub his wife for being the finest untrained retriever in the world. Yes, sir, that's what she is — a retriever; faithful, clever, absolutely unscarable, with no other object in life except to track down and fetch to her husband every possible interesting fact in the world that he don't already know. And then she's so excited and pleased with what she's got in her mouth that it 'most breaks her heart if her man don't seem to care about it. Now, the secret of training her lies in the fact that she won't never trouble to hunt out and fetch you any news that she sees you already know. And just as soon as a man once appreciates all this — then Joy is come to the Home!

"Now there's Ella, for instance," continued the Traveling Salesman thoughtfully. "Ella's a traveling man, too. Sells shotguns up through the Aroostook. Yes, shotguns! Funny, ain't it, and me selling undervests? Ella's an awful smart girl. Good as gold. But cheeky? Oh, my! — Well, once I would have brought her down to the house for Sunday, and advertised her as a 'peach,' and a 'dandy good fellow,' and praised her eyes, and bragged about her cleverness, and generally done my best to smooth over all her little deficiencies with as much palaver as I could. And that little retriever of mine would have gone straight to work and ferreted out every single, solitary, uncomplimentary thing about Ella that she could find, and 'a' fetched 'em to me as pleased and proud as a puppy, expecting, for all the world, to be petted and patted for her astonishing shrewdness. And there would sure have been gloom in the Sabbath.

"But now — now — what I say now is: 'Wife, I'm going to bring Ella down for Sunday. You've never seen her, and you sure will hate her. She's big, and showy, and just a little bit rough sometimes, and she rouges her cheeks too much, and she's likelier than not to chuck me under the chin. But it would help your old man a lot in a business way if you'd be pretty nice to her. And I'm going to send her down here Friday, a day ahead of me.' — And oh, gee! — I ain't any more than jumped off the car Saturday night when there's my little wife out on the street corner with her sweater tied over her head, prancing up and down first on one foot and then on the other — she's so excited, to slip her hand in mine and tell me all about it. 'And Johnny,' she says — even before I've got my glove off — 'Johnny,' she says, 'really, do you know, I think you've done Ella an injustice. Yes, truly I do. Why, she's *just as kind*! And she's shown me how to cut my last year's coat over into the nicest sort of a little spring jacket! And she's made us a chocolate cake as big as a dish-pan. Yes, she has! And Johnny, don't you dare tell her that I told you — but do you know she's putting her brother's boy through Dartmouth? And you old Johnny Clifford, I don't care a darn whether she rouges a little bit or not — and you oughtn't to care — either! So there!'"

With sudden tardy contrition the Salesman's amused eyes wandered to the open book on the Youngish Girl's lap.

"I sure talk too much," he muttered. "I guess maybe you'd like half a chance to read your story."

The expression on the Youngish Girl's face was a curious mixture of humor and seriousness. "There's no special object in reading," she said, "when you can hear a bright man talk!"

As unappreciatingly as a duck might shake champagne from its back, the Traveling Salesman shrugged the compliment from his shoulders.

"Oh, I'm bright enough," he grumbled, "but I ain't refined." Slowly to the tips of his ears mounted a dark red flush of real mortification.

"Now, there's some traveling men," he mourned, "who are as slick and fine as any college president you ever saw. But me? I'd look coarse sipping warm milk out of a gold-lined spoon. I haven't had any education. And I'm fat, besides!" Almost plaintively he turned and stared for a second from the Young Electrician's embarrassed grin to the Youngish Girl's more subtle smile. "Why, I'm nearly fifty years old," he said, "and since I was fifteen the only learning I've ever got was what I picked up in trains talking to whoever sits nearest to me. Sometimes it's hens I learn about. Sometimes it's national politics. Once a young Canuck farmer sitting up all night with me coming down from St. John learned me all about the French Revolution. And now and then high school kids will give me a point or two on astronomy. And in this very seat I'm sitting in now, I guess, a red-kerchiefed Dago woman, who worked on a pansy farm just outside of Boston, used to ride in town with me every night for a month, and she coached me quite a bit on Dago talk, and I paid her five dollars for that."

"Oh, dear me!" said the Youngish Girl, with unmistakable sincerity. "I'm afraid you haven't learned anything at all from me!"

"Oh, yes, I have too!" cried the Traveling Salesman, his whole round face lighting up suddenly with real pleasure. "I've learned about an entirely new kind of lady to go home and tell my wife about. And I'll bet you a hundred dollars that you're a good deal more of a 'lady' than you'd even be willing to tell us. There ain't any provincial — 'Don't-you-dare-speak-to-me — this-is-the-first-time-I-ever-was-on-a-train' air about you! I'll bet you've traveled a lot — all round the world — froze your eyes on icebergs and scorched 'em some on tropics."

"Y-e-s," laughed the Youngish Girl.

"And I'll bet you've met the Governor-General at least once in your life."

"Yes," said the Girl, still laughing. "He dined at my house with me a week ago yesterday."

"And I'll bet you, most of anything," said the Traveling Salesman shrewdly, "that you're haughtier than haughty with folks of your own kind. But with people like us — me and the Electrician, or the soldier's widow from South Africa who does your washing, or the Eskimo man at the circus — you're as simple as a kitten. All your own kind of folks are nothing but grownup people to you, and you treat 'em like grownups all right — a hundred cents to the dollar — but all our kind of folks are *playmates* to you, and you take us as easy and pleasant as you'd slide down on the floor and play with any other kind of a kid. Oh, you can tackle the other proposition all right — dances and balls and general gold lace glories; but it ain't fine loafers sitting round in parlors talking about the weather that's going to hold you very long, when all the time your heart's up and over the back fence with the kids who are playing the games. And, oh, say!" he broke off abruptly — "would you think it awfully impertinent of me if I asked you how you do your hair like that? 'Cause, surer than smoke, after I get home and supper is over and the dishes are washed and I've just got to sleep, that little wife of mine will wake me up and say: 'Oh, just one thing more. How did that lady in the train do her hair?'"

With her chin lifting suddenly in a burst of softly uproarious delight, the Youngish Girl turned her head halfway around and raised her narrow, black-gloved hands to push a tortoise-shell pin into place.

"Why, it's perfectly simple," she explained. "It's just three puffs, and two curls, and then a twist."

"And then a twist?" quizzed the Traveling Salesman earnestly, jotting down the memorandum very carefully on the shiny black surface of his sample-case. "Oh, I hope I ain't been too familiar," he added, with sudden contriteness. "Maybe I ought to have introduced myself first. My name's Clifford. I'm a drummer for Sayles & Sayles. Maine and the Maritime Provinces — that's my route. Boston's the home office. Ever been in Halifax?" he quizzed a trifle proudly. "Do an awful big business in Halifax!

Happen to know the Emporium store? The London, Liverpool, and Halifax Emporium?"

The Youngish Girl bit her lip for a second before she answered. Then, very quietly, "Y-e-s," she said, "I know the Emporium — slightly. That is — I — own the block that the Emporium is in."

"Gee!" said the Traveling Salesman. "Oh, gee! Now I *know* I talk too much!"

In nervously apologetic acquiescence the Young Electrician reached up a lean, clever, mechanical hand and smouched one more streak of black across his forehead in a desperate effort to reduce his tousled yellow hair to the particular smoothness that befitted the presence of a lady who owned a business block in any city whatsoever.

"My father owned a store in Malden, once," he stammered, just a trifle wistfully, "but it burnt down, and there wasn't any insurance. We always were a powerfully unlucky family. Nothing much ever came our way!"

Even as he spoke, a toddling youngster from an overcrowded seat at the front end of the car came adventuring along the aisle after the swaying, clutching manner of tired, fretty children on trains. Hesitating a moment, she stared up utterly unsmilingly into the Salesman's beaming face, ignored the Youngish Girl's inviting hand, and with a sudden little chuckling sigh of contentment, climbed up clumsily into the empty place beside the Young Electrician, rummaged bustlingly around with its hands and feet for an instant, in a petulant effort to make a comfortable nest for itself, and then snuggled down at last, lolling halfway across the Young Electrician's perfectly strange knees, and drowsed off to sleep with all the delicious, friendly, unconcerned sang-froid of a tired puppy. Almost unconsciously the Young Electrician reached out and unfastened the choky collar of the heavy, sweltering little overcoat; yet not a glance from his face had either lured or caressed the strange child for a single second. Just for a moment, then, his smiling eyes reassured the jaded, jabbering French-Canadian mother, who turned round with craning neck from the front of the car.

"She's all right here. Let her alone!" he signaled gesticulatingly from child to mother.

Then, turning to the Traveling Salesman, he mused reminiscently: "Talking's — all — right. But where in creation do you get the time to *think*? Got any kids?" he asked abruptly.

"N-o," said the Traveling Salesman. "My wife, I guess, is kid enough for me."

Around the Young Electrician's eyes the whimsical smile-wrinkles deepened with amazing vividness. "Huh!" he said. "I've got six."

"Gee!" chuckled the Salesman. "Boys?"

The Young Electrician's eyebrows lifted in astonishment. "Sure they're boys!" he said. "Why, of course!"

The Traveling Salesman looked out far away through the window and whistled a long, breathy whistle. "How in the deuce are you ever going to take care of 'em?" he asked. Then his face sobered suddenly. "There was only two of us fellows at home — just Daniel and me — and even so — there weren't ever quite enough of anything to go all the way round."

For just an instant the Youngish Girl gazed a bit skeptically at the Traveling Salesman's general rotund air of prosperity.

"You don't look — exactly like a man who's never had enough," she said smilingly.

"Food?" said the Traveling Salesman. "Oh, shucks! It wasn't food I was thinking of. It was education. Oh, of course," he added conscientiously, "of course, when the crops weren't either too heavy or too blooming light, Pa usually managed some way or other to get Daniel and me to school. And schooling was just nuts to me, and not a single nut so hard or so green that I wouldn't have chawed and bitten my way clear into it. But Daniel — Daniel somehow couldn't seem to see just how to enter a mushy Bartlett pear without a knife or a fork — in some other person's fingers. He was all right, you know — but he just couldn't seem to find his own way alone into anything. So when the time came —" the grin on the Traveling Salesman's mouth grew just a little bit wry at one corner — "and so when the time came — it was an awful nice, sweet-smelling June night, I remember, and I'd come home early — I walked into the kitchen as nice as pie, where Pa was sitting dozing in the cat's rocking-chair, in his gray stocking feet, and I threw down before him my full year's school report. It was pink, I remember, which was supposed to be the rosy color of success in our school; and I says: 'Pa! There's my report! And Pa,' I says, as bold and stuck-up as a brass weathercock on a new church, 'Pa! Teacher says that one of your boys has got to go to college!' And I was grinning all the while, I remember, worse than any Chessy cat.

"And Pa he took my report in both his horny old hands and he spelt it all out real careful and slow and respectful, like as though it had been a lace valentine, and 'Good boy!' he says, and 'Bully boy!' and 'So Teacher says that one of my boys has got to go to college? One of my boys? Well, which one? Go fetch me Daniel's report.' So I went and fetched him Daniel's report. It was gray, I remember — the supposed color of failure in our school — and I stood with the grin still half frozen on my face while Pa spelt out the dingy record of poor Daniel's year. And then, 'Oh, gorry!' says Pa. 'Run away and g'long to bed. I've got to think. But first,' he says, all suddenly cautious and thrifty, 'how much does it cost to go to college?' And just about as delicate and casual as a missionary hinting for a new chapel, I blurted out loud as a bull: 'Well, if I go up state to our own college, and get a chance to work for part of my board, it will cost me just $255 a year, or maybe — maybe,' I stammered, 'maybe, if I'm extra careful, only $245.50, say. For four years that's only $982,' I finished triumphantly.

"'G-a-w-d!' says Pa. Nothing at all except just, 'G-a-w-d!'

"When I came down to breakfast the next morning, he was still sitting there in the cat's rocking-chair, with his face as gray as his socks, and all the rest of him — blue jeans. And my pink school report, I remember, had slipped down under the stove, and the tortoise-shell cat was lashing it with her tail; but Daniel's report, gray as his face, was still clutched up in Pa's horny old hand. For just a second we eyed each other sort of dumb-like, and then for the first time, I tell you, I seen tears in his eyes.

"'Johnny,' he says, 'it's Daniel that'll have to go to college. Bright men,' he says, 'don't need no education.'"

Even after thirty years the Traveling Salesman's hand shook slightly with the memory, and his joggled mind drove him with unwonted carelessness to pin price mark after price mark in the same soft, flimsy mesh of pink lisle. But the grin on his lips did not altogether falter.

"I'd had pains before in my stomach," he acknowledged good-naturedly, "but that morning with Pa was the first time in my life that I ever had any pain in my plans! — So we mortgaged the house and the cow-barn and the maple-sugar trees," he continued, more and more cheerfully, "and Daniel finished his schooling — in the Lord's own time — and went to college."

With another sudden, loud guffaw of mirth all the color came flushing back again into his heavy face.

"Well, Daniel has sure needed all the education he could get," he affirmed heartily. "He's a Methodist minister now somewhere down in Georgia — and, educated 'way up to the top notch, he don't make no more than $650 a year. $650! — oh, glory! Why, Daniel's piazza on his new house cost him $175, and his wife's last hospital bill was $250, and just one dentist alone gaffed him sixty-five dollars for straightening his oldest girl's teeth!"

"Not sixty-five?" gasped the Young Electrician in acute dismay. "Why, two of my kids have got to have it done! Oh, come now — you're joshing!"

"I'm not either joshing," cried the Traveling Salesman. "Sure it was sixty-five dollars. Here's the receipted bill for it right here in my pocket." Brusquely he reached out and snatched the paper back again. "Oh, no, I beg your pardon. That's the receipt for the piazza. — What? It isn't? For the hospital bill then? — Oh, hang! Well, never mind. It *was* sixty-five dollars. I tell you I've got it somewhere."

"Oh — you — paid — for — them — all, did you?" quizzed the Youngish Girl before she had time to think.

"No, indeed!" lied the Traveling Salesman loyally. "But $650 a year? What can a family man do with that? Why, I earned that much before I was twenty-one! Why, there wasn't a moment after I quit school and went to work that I wasn't earning real money! From the first night I stood on a street corner with a gasoline torch, hawking rasin-seeders, up to last night when I got an eight-hundred-dollar raise in my salary, there ain't been a single moment in my life when I couldn't have sold you my boots; and if you'd buncoed my boots away from me I'd have sold you my stockings; and if you'd buncoed my stockings away from me I'd have rented you the privilege of jumping on my bare toes. And I ain't never missed a meal yet — though once in my life I was forty-eight hours late for one! — Oh, I'm bright enough," he mourned, "but I tell you I ain't refined."

With the sudden stopping of the train the little child in the Young Electrician's lap woke fretfully. Then, as the bumpy cars switched laboriously into a siding, and the engine went puffing off alone on some noncommittal errand of its own, the Young Electrician rose and stretched himself and peered out of the window into the acres and acres of snow, and bent down suddenly and swung the child to his shoulder, then, sauntering down the aisle to the door, jumped off into the snow and started to explore the edge of a little, snow-smothered pond which a score of red-mittened children were trying frantically to clear with huge yellow brooms. Out from the crowd of loafers that hung about the station a lean yellow hound came nosing aimlessly forward, and then suddenly, with much fawning and many capers, annexed itself to the Young Electrician's heels like a dog that has just rediscovered its long-lost master. Halfway up the car the French Canadian mother and her brood of children crowded their faces close to the window — and thought they were watching the snow.

And suddenly the car seemed very empty. The Youngish Girl thought it was her book that had grown so astonishingly devoid of interest. Only the Traveling Salesman seemed to know just exactly what was the matter. Craning his neck till his ears reddened, he surveyed and resurveyed the car, complaining: "What's become of all the folks?"

A little nervously the Youngish Girl began to laugh. "Nobody has gone," she said, "except — the Young Electrician."

With a grunt of disbelief the Traveling Salesman edged over to the window and peered out through the deepening frost on the pane. Inquisitively the Youngish Girl followed his gaze. Already across the cold, white, monotonous, snow-smothered landscape the pale afternoon light was beginning to wane, and against the lowering red and purple streaks of the wintry sunset the Young Electrician's figure, with the little huddling pack on its shoulder, was silhouetted vaguely, with an almost startling mysticism, like the figure of an unearthly Traveler starting forth upon an unearthly journey into an unearthly West.

"Ain't he the nice boy!" exclaimed the Traveling Salesman with almost passionate vehemence.

"Why, I'm sure I don't know!" said the Youngish Girl a trifle coldly. "Why — it would take me quite a long time — to decide just how — nice he was. But —" with a quick softening of her voice — "but he certainly makes one think of — nice things — Blue Mountains, and Green Forests, and Brown Pine Needles, and a Long, Hard Trail, shoulder to shoulder — with a chance to warm one's heart at last at a hearth-fire — bigger than a sunset!"

Altogether unconsciously her small hands went gripping out to the edge of her seat, as though just a grip on plush could hold her imagination back from soaring into a miraculous, unfamiliar world where women did not idle all day long on carpets waiting for men who came on — pavements.

"Oh, my God!" she cried out with sudden passion. "I wish I could have lived just one day when the world was new. I wish — I wish I could have reaped just one single, solitary, big Emotion before the world had caught it and — appraised it — and taxed it — and licensed it — and *staled* it!"

"Oh-ho!" said the Traveling Salesman with a little sharp indrawing of his breath. "Oh-ho! — So that's what the — Young Electrician makes you think of, is it?"

For just an instant the Traveling Salesman thought that the Youngish Girl was going to strike him.

"I wasn't thinking of the Young Electrician at all!" she asserted angrily. "I was thinking of something altogether — different."

"Yes. That's just it," murmured the Traveling Salesman placidly. "Something — altogether — different. Every time I look at him it's the darnedest thing! Every time I look at him I — forget all about him. My head begins to wag and my foot begins to tap — and I find myself trying to — *hum* him — as though he was the words of a tune I used to know."

When the Traveling Salesman looked round again, there were tears in the Youngish Girl's eyes, and an instant after that her shoulders went plunging forward till her forehead rested on the back of the Traveling Salesman's seat.

But it was not until the Young Electrician had come striding back to his seat, and wrapped himself up in the fold of a big newspaper, and not until the train had started on again and had ground out another noisy mile or so, that the Traveling Salesman spoke again — and this time it was just a little bit surreptitiously.

"What — you — crying — for?" he asked with incredible gentleness.

"I don't know, I'm sure," confessed the Youngish Girl, snuffingly. "I guess I must be tired."

"U-m-m," said the Traveling Salesman.

After a moment or two he heard the sharp little click of a watch.

"Oh, dear me!" fretted the Youngish Girl's somewhat smothered voice. "I didn't realize we were almost two hours late. Why, it will be dark, won't it, when we get into Boston?"

"Yes, sure it will be dark," said the Traveling Salesman.

After another moment the Youngish Girl raised her forehead just the merest trifle from the back of the Traveling Salesman's seat, so that her voice sounded distinctly more definite and cheerful. "I've — never — been — to — Boston — before," she drawled a little casually.

"What!" exclaimed the Traveling Salesman. "Been all around the world — and never been to Boston? — Oh, I see," he added hurriedly, "you're afraid your friends won't meet you!"

Out of the Youngish Girl's erstwhile disconsolate mouth a most surprising laugh issued. "No! I'm afraid they *will* meet me," she said dryly.

Just as a soldier's foot turns from his heel alone, so the Traveling Salesman's whole face seemed to swing out suddenly from his chin, till his surprised eyes stared direct into the Girl's surprised eyes.

"My heavens!" he said. "You don't mean that *you've* — been writing an — 'indiscreet letter'?"

"Y-e-s — I'm afraid that I have," said the Youngish Girl quite blandly. She sat up very straight now and narrowed her eyes just a trifle stubbornly toward the Traveling Salesman's very visible astonishment. "And what's more," she continued, clicking at her watch-case again — "and what's more, I'm on my way now to meet the consequences of said indiscreet letter.'"

"Alone?" gasped the Traveling Salesman.

The twinkle in the Youngish Girl's eyes brightened perceptibly, but the firmness did not falter from her mouth.

"Are people apt to go in — crowds to — meet consequences?" she asked, perfectly pleasantly.

"Oh — come, now!" said the Traveling Salesman's most persuasive voice. "You don't want to go and get mixed up in any sensational nonsense and have your picture stuck in the Sunday paper, do you?"

The Youngish Girl's manner stiffened a little. "Do I look like a person who gets mixed up in sensational nonsense?" she demanded rather sternly.

"N-o-o," acknowledged the Traveling Salesman conscientiously. "N-o-o; but then there's never any telling what you calm, quiet-looking, still-waters sort of people will go ahead and do — once you get started." Anxiously he took out his watch, and then began hurriedly to pack his samples back into his case. "It's only twenty-five minutes more," he argued earnestly. "Oh, I say now, don't you go off and do anything foolish! My wife will be down at the station to meet me. You'd like my wife. You'd like her fine! — Oh, I say now, you come home with us for Sunday, and think things over a bit."

As delightedly as when the Traveling Salesman had asked her how she fixed her hair, the Youngish Girl's hectic nervousness broke into genuine laughter. "Yes," she teased, "I can see just how pleased your wife would be to have you bring home a perfectly strange lady for Sunday!"

"My wife is only a kid," said the Traveling Salesman gravely, "but she likes what I like — all right — and she'd give you the shrewdest, eagerest little 'helping hand' that you ever got in your life — if you'd only give her a chance to help you out — with whatever your trouble is."

"But I haven't any 'trouble,'" persisted the Youngish Girl with brisk cheerfulness. "Why, I haven't any trouble at all! Why, I don't know but what I'd just as soon tell you all about it. Maybe I really ought to tell somebody about it. Maybe — anyway, it's a good deal easier to tell a stranger than a friend. Maybe it would really do me good to hear how it sounds out loud. You see, I've never done anything but whisper it — just to myself — before. Do you remember the wreck on the Canadian Pacific Road last year? Do you? Well — I was in it!"

"Gee!" said the Traveling Salesman. "'Twas up on just the edge of Canada, wasn't it? And three of the passenger coaches went off the track? And the sleeper went clear over the bridge?

And fell into an awful gully? And caught fire besides?"

"Yes," said the Youngish Girl. "I was in the sleeper."

Even without seeming to look at her at all, the Traveling Salesman could see quite distinctly that the Youngish Girl's knees were fairly knocking together and that the flesh around her mouth was suddenly gray and drawn, like an old person's. But the little persistent desire to laugh off everything still flickered about the corners of her lips.

"Yes," she said, "I was in the sleeper, and the two people right in front of me were killed; and it took almost three hours, I think, before they got any of us out. And while I was lying there in the darkness and mess and everything, I cried — and cried — and cried. It wasn't nice of me, I know, nor brave, nor anything, but I couldn't seem to help it — underneath all that pile of broken seats and racks and beams and things.

"And pretty soon a man's voice — just a voice, no face or anything, you know, but just a voice from somewhere quite near me, spoke right out and said: 'What in creation are you crying so about? Are you awfully hurt?' And I said — though I didn't mean to say it at all, but it came right out — 'N-o, I don't think I'm hurt, but I don't like having all these seats and windows piled on top of me,' and I began crying all over again. 'But no one else is crying,' reproached the Voice. — 'And there's a perfectly good reason why not,' I said. 'They're all dead!' — 'O-h-h,' said the Voice, and then I began to cry harder than ever, and principally this time, I think, I cried because the horrid, old red plush cushions smelt so stale and dusty, jammed against my nose.

"And then after a long time the Voice spoke again and it said, 'If I'll sing you a little song, will you stop crying?' And I said, 'N-o, I don't think I could!' And after a long time the Voice spoke again, and it said, 'Well, if I'll tell you a story will you stop crying?' And I considered it a long time, and finally I said, 'Well, if you'll tell me a perfectly true story — a story that's never, never been told to any one before — *I'll try and stop!*

"So the Voice gave a funny little laugh almost like a woman's hysterics, and I stopped crying right off short, and the Voice said, just a little bit mockingly: 'But the only perfectly true story that I know — the only story that's never — never been told to anybody before is the story of my life.' 'Very well, then,' I said, 'tell me that!

Of course I was planning to live to be very old and learn a little about a great many things; but as long as apparently I'm not going to live to even reach my twenty-ninth birthday — to-morrow — you don't know how unutterably it would comfort me to think that at least I knew *everything* about some one thing!'

"And then the Voice choked again, just a little bit, and said: 'Well — here goes, then. Once upon a time — but first, can you move your right hand? Turn it just a little bit more this way. There! Cuddle it down! Now, you see, I've made a little home for it in mine. Ouch! Don't press down too hard! I think my wrist is broken. All ready, then? You won't cry another cry? Promise? All right then. Here goes. Once upon a time —'

"Never mind about the story," said the Youngish Girl tersely. "It began about the first thing in all his life that he remembered seeing — something funny about a grandmother's brown wig hung over the edge of a white piazza railing — and he told me his name and address, and all about his people, and all about his business, and what banks his money was in, and something about some land down in the Panhandle, and all the bad things that he'd ever done in his life, and all the good things, that he wished there'd been more of, and all the things that no one would dream of telling you if he ever, ever expected to see Daylight again — things so intimate — things so —

"But it wasn't, of course, about his story that I wanted to tell you. It was about the 'home,' as he called it, that his broken hand made for my — frightened one. I don't know how to express it; I can't exactly think, even, of any words to explain it. Why, I've been all over the world, I tell you, and fairly loafed and lolled in every conceivable sort of ease and luxury, but the Soul of me — the wild, restless, breathless, discontented *soul* of me — *never sat down before in all its life* — I say, until my frightened hand cuddled into his broken one. I tell you I don't pretend to explain it, I don't pretend to account for it; all I know is — that smothering there under all that horrible wreckage and everything — the instant my hand went home to his, the most absolute sense of serenity and contentment went over me. Did you ever see young white horses straying through a white-birch wood in the spring-time? Well, it felt the way that *looks*! — Did you ever hear an alto voice singing in the candle-light? Well, it felt the way that *sounds*!

The last vision you would like to glut your eyes on before blindness smote you! The last sound you would like to glut your ears on before deafness dulled you! The last touch — before Intangibility! Something final, complete, supreme — ineffably satisfying!

"And then people came along and rescued us, and I was sick in the hospital for several weeks. And then after that I went to Persia. I know it sounds silly, but it seemed to me as though just the smell of Persia would be able to drive away even the memory of red plush dust and scorching woodwork. And there was a man on the steamer whom I used to know at home — a man who's almost always wanted to marry me. And there was a man who joined our party at Teheran — who liked me a little. And the land was like silk and silver and attar of roses. But all the time I couldn't seem to think about anything except how perfectly awful it was that a *stranger* like me should be running round loose in the world, carrying all the big, scary secrets of a man who didn't even know where I was. And then it came to me all of a sudden, one rather worrisome day, that no woman who knew as much about a man as I did was exactly a 'stranger' to him. And then, twice as suddenly, to great, grownup, cool-blooded, money-staled, book-tamed *me* — it swept over me like a cyclone that I should never be able to decide anything more in all my life — not the width of a tinsel ribbon, not the goal of a journey, not the worth of a lover — until I'd seen the Face that belonged to the Voice in the railroad wreck.

"And I sat down — and wrote the man a letter — I had his name and address, you know. And there — in a rather maddening moonlight night on the Caspian Sea — all the horrors and terrors of that other — Canadian night came back to me and swamped completely all the arid timidity and sleek conventionality that women like me are hidebound with all their lives, and I wrote him — that unknown, unvisualized, unimagined — man — the utterly free, utterly frank, utterly honest sort of letter that any brave soul would write any other brave soul — every day of the world — if there wasn't any flesh. It wasn't a love letter. It wasn't even a sentimental letter. Never mind what I told him. Never mind anything except that there, in that tropical night on a moonlit sea, I asked him to meet me here, in Boston, eight months afterward — on the same Boston-bound Canadian train — on this — the anniversary of our other tragic meeting."

"And you think he'll be at the station?" gasped the Traveling Salesman.

The Youngish Girl's answer was astonishingly tranquil. "I don't know, I'm sure," she said. "That part of it isn't my business. All I know is that I wrote the letter — and mailed it. It's Fate's move next."

"But maybe he never got the letter!" protested the Traveling Salesman, buckling frantically at the straps of his sample-case.

"Very likely," the Youngish Girl answered calmly. "And if he never got it, then Fate has surely settled everything perfectly definitely for me — that way. The only trouble with that would be," she added whimsically, "that an unanswered letter is always pretty much like an unhooked hook. Any kind of a gap is apt to be awkward, and the hook that doesn't catch in its own intended tissue is mighty apt to tear later at something you didn't want torn."

"I don't know anything about that," persisted the Traveling Salesman, brushing nervously at the cinders on his hat. "All I say is — maybe he's married."

"Well, that's all right," smiled the Youngish Girl. "Then Fate would have settled it all for me perfectly satisfactorily *that* way. I wouldn't mind at all his not being at the station. And I wouldn't mind at all his being married. And I wouldn't mind at all his turning out to be very, very old. None of those things, you see, would interfere in the slightest with the memory of the — Voice or the — chivalry of the broken hand. The only thing i'd mind, i tell you, would be to think that he really and truly was the man who was made for me — and i missed finding it out! — Oh, of course, I've worried myself sick these past few months thinking of the audacity of what I've done. I've got such a 'Sore Thought,' as you call it, that I'm almost ready to scream if anybody mentions the word 'indiscreet' in my presence. And yet, and yet — after all, it isn't as though I were reaching out into the darkness after an indefinite object. What I'm reaching out for is a *light*, so that I can tell exactly just what object is there. And, anyway," she quoted a little waveringly:

"He either fears his fate too much,"

Or his, deserts are small,
Who dares not put it to the touch
To gain or lose it all!"

"Ain't you scared just a little bit?" probed the Traveling Salesman.

All around them the people began bustling suddenly with their coats and bags. With a gesture of impatience the Youngish Girl jumped up and started to fasten her furs. The eyes that turned to answer the Traveling Salesman's question were brimming wet with tears.

"Yes — I'm — scared to death!" she smiled incongruously.

Almost authoritatively the Salesman reached out his empty hand for her traveling-bag. "What you going to do if he ain't there?" he asked.

The Girl's eyebrows lifted. "Why, just what I'm going to do if he *is* there," she answered quite definitely. "I'm going right back to Montreal tonight. There's a train out again, I think, at eight-thirty. Even late as we are, that will give me an hour and a half at the station."

"Gee!" said the Traveling Salesman. "And you've traveled five days just to see what a man looks like — for an hour and a half?"

"I'd have traveled twice five days," she whispered, "just to see what he looked like — for a — second and a half!"

"But how in thunder are you going to recognize him?" fussed the Traveling Salesman. "And how in thunder is he going to recognize you?"

"Maybe I won't recognize him," acknowledged the Youngish Girl, "and likelier than not he won't recognize me; but don't you see? — can't you understand? — that all the audacity of it, all the worry of it — is absolutely nothing compared to the one little chance in ten thousand that we *will* recognize each other?"

"Well, anyway," said the Traveling Salesman stubbornly, "I'm going to walk out slow behind you and see you through this thing all right."

"Oh, no, you're not!" exclaimed the Youngish Girl. "Oh, no, you're not! Can't you see that if he's there, I wouldn't mind you so much; but if he doesn't come, can't you understand that maybe I'd just as soon you didn't know about it?"

"O-h," said the Traveling Salesman.

A little impatiently he turned and routed the Young Electrician out of his sprawling nap. "Don't you know Boston when you see it?" he cried a trifle testily.

For an instant the Young Electrician's sleepy eyes stared dully into the Girl's excited face. Then he stumbled up a bit awkwardly and reached out for all his coil-boxes and insulators.

"Good-night to you. Much obliged to you," he nodded amiably.

A moment later he and the Traveling Salesman were forging their way ahead through the crowded aisle. Like the transient, impersonal, altogether mysterious stimulant of a strain of martial music, the Young Electrician vanished into space. But just at the edge of the car steps the Traveling Salesman dallied a second to wait for the Youngish Girl.

"Say," he said, "say, can I tell my wife what you've told me?"

"Y-e-s," nodded the Youngish Girl soberly.

"And say," said the Traveling Salesman, "say, I don't exactly like to go off this way and never know at all how it all came out." Casually his eyes fell on the big lynx muff in the Youngish Girl's hand. "Say," he said, "if I promise, honest-Injun, to go 'way off to the other end of the station, couldn't you just lift your muff up high, once, if everything comes out the way you want it?"

"Y-e-s," whispered the Youngish Girl almost inaudibly.

Then the Traveling Salesman went hurrying on to join the Young Electrician, and the Youngish Girl lagged along on the rear edge of the crowd like a bashful child dragging on the skirts of its mother.

Out of the groups of impatient people that flanked the track she saw a dozen little pecking reunions, where some one dashed wildly into the long, narrow stream of travelers and yanked out his special friend or relative, like a good-natured bird of prey. She saw a tired, worn, patient-looking woman step forward with four noisy little boys, and then stand dully waiting while the Young Electrician gathered his riotous offspring to his breast. She saw the Traveling Salesman grin like a bashful schoolboy, just as a red-cloaked girl came running to him and bore him off triumphantly toward the street.

And then suddenly, out of the blur, and the dust, and the dizziness, and the half-blinding glare of lights, the figure of a Man loomed up directly and indomitably across the Youngish Girl's path — a Man standing bare-headed and faintly smiling as one who welcomes a much-reverenced guest — a Man tall, stalwart, sober-eyed, with a touch of gray at his temples, a Man whom any woman would be proud to have waiting for her at the end of any journey. And right there before all that hurrying, scurrying, self-centered, unseeing crowd, he reached out his hands to her and gathered her frightened fingers close into his.

"You've — kept — me — waiting — a — long — time," he reproached her.

"Yes!" she stammered. "Yes! Yes! The train was two hours late!"

"It wasn't the hours that I was thinking about," said the Man very quietly. "It was the — *year!*"

And then, just as suddenly, the Youngish Girl felt a tug at her coat, and, turning round quickly, found herself staring with dazed eyes into the eager, childish face of the Traveling Salesman's red-cloaked wife. Not thirty feet away from her the Traveling Sales-man's shameless, stolid-looking back seemed to be blocking up the main exit to the street.

"Oh, are you the lady from British Columbia?" queried the excited little voice. Perplexity, amusement, yet a divine sort of marital confidence were in the question.

"Yes, surely I am," said the Youngish Girl softly.

Across the little wife's face a great rushing, flushing wave of tenderness blocked out for a second all trace of the cruel, slim scar that marred the perfect contour of one cheek.

"Oh, I don't know at all what it's all about," laughed the little wife, "but my husband asked me to come back and kiss you!"

LITTLE EVE EDGARTON

CHAPTER I

"But you live like such a fool — of course you're bored!" drawled the Older Man, rummaging listlessly through his pockets for the ever-elusive match.

"Well, I like your nerve!" protested the Younger Man with unmistakable asperity.

"Do you — really?" mocked the Older Man, still smiling very faintly.

For a few minutes then both men resumed their cigars, staring blinkishly out all the while from their dark green piazza corner into the dazzling white tennis courts that gleamed like so many slippery pine planks in the afternoon glare and heat. The month was August, the day typically handsome, typically vivid, typically caloric.

It was the Younger Man who recovered his conversational interest first. "So you think I'm a fool?" he resumed at last quite abruptly.

"Oh, no — no! Not for a minute!" denied the Older Man. "Why, my dear sir, I never even implied that you were a fool! All I said was that you — lived like a fool!"

Starting to be angry, the Younger Man laughed instead. "You're certainly rather an amusing sort of chap," he acknowledged reluctantly.

A gleam of real pride quickened most ingenuously in the Older Man's pale blue eyes. "Why, that's just the whole point of my argument," he beamed. "Now — you look interesting. But you aren't! And I — don't look interesting. But it seems that I am!"

"You — you've got a nerve!" reverted the Younger Man.

Altogether serenely the Older Man began to rummage again through all his pockets. "Thank you for your continuous compliments," he mused. "Thank you, I say. Thank you — very much. Now for the very first time, sir, it's beginning to dawn on me just why you have honored me with so much of your company — the past three or four days. I truly believe that you like me! Eh? But up to last Monday, if I remember correctly," he added drily, "it was that showy young Philadelphia crowd that was absorbing the larger part of your — valuable attention? Eh? Wasn't it?"

"What in thunder are you driving at?" snapped the Younger Man. "What are you trying to string me about, anyway? What's the harm if I did say that I wished to glory I'd never come to this blasted hotel? Of all the stupid people! Of all the stupid places! Of all the stupid — everything!"

"The mountains here are considered quite remarkable by some," suggested the Older Man blandly.

"Mountains?" snarled the Younger Man. "Mountains? Do you think for a moment that a fellow like me comes to a God-forsaken spot like this for the sake of mountains?"

A trifle noisily the Older Man jerked his chair around and, slouching down into his shabby gray clothes, with his hands thrust deep into his pockets, his feet shoved out before him, sat staring at his companion. Furrowed abruptly from brow to chin with myriad infinitesimal wrinkles of perplexity, his lean, droll face looked suddenly almost monkeyish in its intentness.

"What does a fellow like you come to a place like this for?" he asked bluntly.

"Why — tennis," conceded the Younger Man. "A little tennis. And golf — a little golf. And — and —"

"And — girls," asserted the Older Man with precipitous conviction.

Across the Younger Man's splendidly tailored shoulders a little flicker of self-consciousness went crinkling. "Oh, of course," he grinned. "Oh, of course I've got a vacationist's usual partiality for pretty girls. But Great Heavens!" he began, all over again. "Of all the stupid — !"

"But you live like such a fool — of course you're bored," resumed the Older Man.

"There you are at it again!" stormed the Younger Man with tempestuous resentment.

"Why shouldn't I be 'at it again'?" argued the Older Man mildly. "Always and forever picking out the showiest people that you can find — and always and forever being bored to death with them eventually, but never learning anything from it — that's you! Now wouldn't that just naturally suggest to any observing stranger that there was something radically idiotic about your method of life?"

"But that Miss Von Eaton looked like such a peach!" protested the Younger Man worriedly.

"That's exactly what I say," droned the Older Man.

"Why, she's the handsomest girl here!" insisted the Younger Man arrogantly.

"That's exactly what I say," droned the Older Man.

"And the best dresser!" boasted the Younger Man stubbornly.

"That's exactly what I say," droned the Older Man.

"Why, just that pink paradise hat alone would have knocked almost any chap silly," grinned the Younger Man a bit sheepishly.

"Humph!" mused the Older Man still droningly. "Humph! When a chap falls in love with a girl's hat at a summer resort, what he ought to do is to hike back to town on the first train he can catch — and go find the milliner who made the hat!"

"Hike back to — town?" gibed the Younger Man. "Ha!" he sneered. "A chap would have to hike back a good deal farther than 'town' these days to find a girl that was worth hiking back for! What in thunder's the matter with all the girls?" he queried petulantly. "They get stupider and stupider every summer! Why, the peachiest débutante you meet the whole season can't hold your interest much beyond the stage where you once begin to call her by her first name!"

Irritably, as he spoke, he reached out for a bright-covered magazine from the great pile of books and papers that sprawled on the wicker table close at his elbow. "Where in blazes do the storybook writers find their girls?" he demanded. Noisily with his knuckles he began to knock through page after page of the magazine's big-typed advertisements concerning the year's most popular storybook heroines. "Why — here are no end of storybook girls," he complained, "that could keep a fellow guessing till his hair was nine shades of white! Look at the corking things they say! But what earthly good are any of 'em to you? They're not real! Why, there was a little girl in a magazine story last month —! Why, I could have died for her! But confound it, I say, what's the use? They're none of 'em real! Nothing but moonshine! Nothing in the world, I tell you, but just plain made-up moonshine! Absolutely improbable!"

Slowly the Older Man drew in his long, rambling legs and

crossed one knee adroitly over the other.

"Improbable — your grandmother!" said the Older Man. "If there's — one person on the face of this earth who makes me sick it's the ninny who calls a thing 'improbable' because it happens to be outside his own special, puny experience of life."

Tempestuously the Younger Man slammed down his magazine to the floor.

"Great Heavens, man!" he demanded. "Where in thunder would a fellow like me start out to find a storybook girl? A real girl, I mean!"

"Almost anywhere — outside yourself," murmured the Older Man blandly.

"Eh?" jerked the Younger Man.

"That's what I said," drawled the Older Man with unruffled suavity. "But what's the use?" he added a trifle more briskly. "Though you searched a thousand years! A 'real girl'? Bah! You wouldn't know a 'real girl' if you saw her!"

"I tell you I would!" snapped the Younger Man.

"I tell you — you wouldn't!" said the Older Man.

"Prove it!" challenged the Younger Man.

"It's already proved!" confided the Older Man. "Ha! I know your type!" he persisted frankly. "You're the sort of fellow, at a party, who just out of sheer fool-instinct will go trampling down every other man in sight just for the sheer fool-joy of trying to get the first dance with the most conspicuously showy-looking, most conspicuously artificial-looking girl in the room — who always and invariably 'bores you to death' before the evening is over! And while you and the rest of your kind are battling together — year after year — for this special privilege of being 'bored to death,' the 'real girl' that you're asking about, the marvelous girl, the girl with the big, beautiful, unspoken thoughts in her head, the girl with the big, brave, undone deeds in her heart, the girl that stories are made of, the girl whom you call 'improbable' — is moping off alone in some dark, cold corner — or sitting forlornly partnerless against the bleak wall of the ballroom — or hiding shyly up in the dressing-room — waiting to be discovered! Little Miss Still-Waters, deeper than ten thousand seas! Little Miss Gunpowder, milder than the dusk before the moon ignites it! Little Miss Sleeping-Beauty, waiting for her Prince!"

"Oh, yes — I suppose so," conceded the Younger Man impatiently. "But that Miss Von Eaton —"

"Oh, it isn't that I don't know a pretty face — or hat, when I see it," interrupted the Older Man nonchalantly. "It's only that I don't put my trust in 'em." With a quick gesture, half audacious, half apologetic, he reached forward suddenly and tapped the Younger Man's coat sleeve. "Oh, I knew just as well as you," he affirmed, "oh, I knew just as well as you — at my first glance — that your gorgeous young Miss Von Eaton was excellingly handsome. But I also knew — not later certainly than my second glance — that she was presumably rather stupid. You can't be interesting, you know, my young friend, unless you do interesting things — and handsome creatures are proverbially lazy. Humph! If Beauty is excuse enough for Being, it sure takes Plainness then to feel the real necessity for — Doing.

"So, speaking of hats, if it's stimulating conversation that you're after, if you're looking for something unique, something significant, something really worth while — what you want to do, my young friend, is to find a girl with a hat you'd be ashamed to go out with — and stay home with her! That's where you'll find the brains, the originality, the vivacity, the sagacity, the real ideas!"

With his first sign of genuine amusement the Younger Man tipped back his head and laughed right up into the green-lined roof of the piazza. "Now just whom would you specially recommend for me?" he demanded mirthfully. "Among all the feminine galaxy of bores and frumps that seem to be congregated at this particular hotel — just whom would you specially recommend for me? The stoop-shouldered, schoolmarmy Botany dame with her incessant garden gloves? Or? — Or — ?" His whole face brightened suddenly with a rather extraordinary amount of humorous malice: "Or how about that duddy-looking little Edgarton girl that I saw you talking with this morning?" he asked delightedly. "Heaven knows she's colorless enough to suit even you — with her winter-before-spring-before-summer-before-last clothes and her voice so meek you'd have to hold her in your lap to hear it. And her —"

"That 'duddy-looking' little Miss Edgarton — meek?" mused the Older Man in sincere astonishment. "Meek? Why, man alive, she was born in a snow-shack on the Yukon River! She was at

Pekin in the Boxer Rebellion! She's roped steers in Oklahoma! She's matched her embroidery silks to all the sunrise tints on the Himalayas! Just why in creation should she seem meek — do you suppose — to a — to a — twenty-five-dollar-a-week clerk like yourself?"

"'A twenty-five-dollar-a-week clerk like myself?'" the Younger Man fairly gasped. "Why — why — I'm the junior partner of the firm of Barton & Barton, stock-brokers! Why, we're the biggest —"

"Is that so?" quizzed the Older Man with feigned surprise. "Well — well — well! I beg your pardon. But now doesn't it all go to prove just exactly what I said in the beginning — that it doesn't behoove a single one of us to judge too hastily by appearances?"

As if fairly overwhelmed with embarrassment he sat staring silently off into space for several seconds. Then — "Speaking of this Miss Edgarton," he resumed genially, "have you ever exactly sought her out — as it were — and actually tried to get acquainted with her?"

"No," said Barton shortly. "Why, the girl must be thirty years old!"

"S-o-o?" mused the Older Man. "Just about your age?"

"I'm thirty-two," growled the Younger Man.

"I'm sixty-two, thank God!" acknowledged the Older Man. "And your gorgeous Miss Von Eaton — who bores you so — all of a sudden — is about — ?"

"Twenty," prompted the Younger Man.

"Poor — senile — babe," ruminated the Older Man soberly,

"Eh?" gasped the Younger Man, edging forward in his chair. "Eh? 'Senile'? Twenty?"

"Sure!" grinned the Older Man. "Twenty is nothing but the 'sere and yellow leaf' of infantile caprice! But thirty is the jocund youth of character! On land or sea the Lord Almighty never made anything as radiantly, divinely young as — thirty! Oh, but thirty's the darling age in a woman!" he added with sudden exultant positiveness. "Thirty's the birth of individuality! Thirty's the —"

"Twenty has got quite enough individuality for me, thank you!" asserted Barton with some curtness.

"But it hasn't!" cried the Older Man hotly. "You've just confessed that it hasn't!" In an amazing impulse of protest he reached out and shook his freckled fist right under the Younger Man's nose. "Twenty, I tell you, hasn't got any individuality at all!" he persisted vehemently.

"Twenty isn't anything at all except the threadbare cloak of her father's idiosyncrasies, lined with her mother's made-over tact, trimmed with her great-aunt somebody's short-lipped smile, shrouding a brand-new frame of — God knows what!"

"Eh? What?" questioned the Younger Man uneasily.

"When a girl is twenty, I tell you," persisted the Older Man — "there's not one marrying man among us — Heaven help us! — who can swear whether her charm is Love's own permanent food or just Nature's temporary bait! At twenty, I tell you, there's not one man among us who can prove whether vivacity is temperament or just plain kiddishness; whether sweetness is real disposition or just coquetry; whether tenderness is personal discrimination or just sex; whether dumbness is stupidity or just brain hoarding its immature treasure; whether indeed coldness is prudery or just conscious passion banking its fires! The dear daredevil sweetheart whom you worship at eighteen will evolve, likelier than not, into a mighty sour prig at forty; and the dove-gray lass who led you to church with her prayer-book ribbons twice every Sunday will very probably decide to go on the vaudeville stage — when her children are just in the high school; and the dull-eyed wallflower whom you dodged at all your college dances will turn out, ten chances to one, the only really wonderful woman you know! But at thirty! Oh, ye gods, Barton! If a girl interests you at thirty you'll be utterly mad about her when she's forty — fifty — sixty! If she's merry at thirty, if she's ardent, if she's tender, it's her own established merriment, it's her own irreducible ardor, it's her — Why, man alive! Why — why —"

"Oh, for Heaven's sake!" gasped Barton. "Whoa there! Go slow! How in creation do you expect anybody to follow you?"

"Follow me? Follow me?" mused the Older Man perplexedly. Staring very hard at Barton, he took the opportunity to swallow rather loudly once or twice.

"Now speaking of Miss Edgarton," he resumed persistently, "now, speaking of this Miss Edgarton, I don't presume for an instant that you're looking for a wife on this trip, but are merely hankering a bit now and then for something rather specially diverting in the line of feminine companionship?"

"Well, what of it?" conceded the Younger Man.

"This of it," argued the Older Man. "If you are really craving the interesting why don't you go out and rummage around for it? Rummage around was what I said! Yes! The real hundred-cent-to-the-dollar treasures of Life, you know, aren't apt to be found labeled as such and lying round very loose on the smugly paved general highway! And astonishingly good looks and astonishingly good clothes are pretty nearly always equivalent to a sign saying, 'I've already been discovered, thank you!' But the really big sport of existence, young man, is to strike out somewhere and discover things for yourself!"

"Is — it?" scoffed Barton.

"It is!" asserted the Older Man. "The woman, I tell you, who fathoms heroism in the fellow that every one else thought was a knave — she's got something to brag about! The fellow who's shrewd enough to spy unutterable lovableness in the woman that no man yet has ever even remotely suspected of being lovable at all — God! It's like being Adam with the whole world virgin!"

"Oh, that may be all right in theory," acknowledged the Younger Man, with some reluctance. "But —"

"Now, speaking of Miss Edgarton," resumed the Older Man monotonously.

"Oh, hang Miss Edgarton!" snapped the Younger Man. "I wouldn't be seen talking to her! She hasn't any looks! She hasn't any style! She hasn't any — anything! Of all the hopelessly plain girls! Of all the — !"

"Now see here, my young friend," begged the Older Man blandly. "The fellow who goes about the world judging women by the sparkle of their eyes or the pink of their cheeks or the sheen of their hair — runs a mighty big risk of being rated as just one of two things, a sensualist or a fool."

"Are you trying to insult me?" demanded the Younger Man furiously.

Freakishly the Older Man twisted his thin-lipped mouth and one glowering eyebrow into a surprisingly sudden and irresistible smile.

"Why — no," he drawled. "Under all existing circumstances I should think I was complimenting you pretty considerably by rating you only as a fool."

"Eh?" jumped Barton again.

"U-m-m," mused the Older Man thoughtfully. "Now believe me, Barton, once and for all, there's no such thing as a 'hopelessly plain woman'! Every woman, I tell you, is beautiful concerning the thing that she's most interested in! And a man's an everlasting dullard who can't ferret out what that interest is and summon its illuminating miracle into an otherwise indifferent face —"

"Is that so?" sniffed Barton.

Lazily the Older Man struggled to his feet and stretched his arms till his bones began to crack.

"Bah! What's beauty, anyway," he complained, "except just a question of where Nature has concentrated her supreme forces — in outgrowing energy, which is beauty; or ingrowing energy, which is brains! Now I like a little good looks as well as anybody," he confided, still yawning, "but when I see a woman living altogether on the outside of her face I don't reckon too positively on there being anything very exciting going on inside that face. So by the same token, when I see a woman who isn't squandering any centric fires at all on the contour of her nose or the arch of her eyebrows or the flesh-tints of her cheeks, it surely does pique my curiosity to know just what wonderful consuming energy she is busy about.

"A face isn't meant to be a living-room, anyway, Barton, but just a piazza where the seething, preoccupied soul can dash out now and then to bask in the breeze and refreshment of sympathy and appreciation. Surely then — it's no particular personal glory to you that your friend Miss Von Eaton's energy cavorts perpetually in the gold of her hair or the blue of her eyes, because rain or shine, congeniality or noncongeniality, her energy hasn't any other place to go. But I tell you it means some compliment to a man when in a bleak, dour, work-worn personality like the old Botany dame's for instance he finds himself able to lure out into occasional facial ecstasy the *amazing* vitality which has been slaving for Science alone these past fifty years. Mushrooms are what the old Botany dame is interested in, Barton. Really, Barton, I think you'd be surprised to see how extraordinarily beautiful the old Botany dame can be about mushrooms! Gleam of the first faint streak of dawn, freshness of the wildest woodland dell, verve of the long day's strenuous effort, flush of sunset and triumph, zeal of the student's evening lamp, puckering, daredevil smile of reckless experiment — "

"Say! Are you a preacher?" mocked the Younger Man sarcastically.

"No more than any old man," conceded the Older Man with unruffled good-nature.

"Old man?" repeated Barton, skeptically. In honest if reluctant admiration for an instant, he sat appraising his companion's extraordinary litheness and agility. "Ha!" he laughed. "It would take a good deal older head than yours to discover what that Miss Edgarton's beauty is!"

"Or a good deal younger one, perhaps," suggested the Older Man judicially. "But — but speaking of Miss Edgarton —" he began all over again.

"Oh — drat Miss Edgarton!" snarled the Younger Man viciously. "You've got Miss Edgarton on the brain! Miss Edgarton this! Miss Edgarton that! Miss Edgarton! Who in blazes is Miss Edgarton, anyway?"

"Miss Edgarton? Miss Edgarton?" mused the Older Man thoughtfully. "Who is she? Miss Edgarton? Why — no one special — except — just my daughter."

Like a fly plunged all unwittingly upon a sheet of sticky paper the Younger Man's hands and feet seemed to shoot out suddenly in every direction.

"Good Heavens!" he gasped. "Your daughter?" he mumbled. "Your daughter?" Every other word or phrase in the English language seemed to be stricken suddenly from his lips. "Your — your — daughter?" he began all over again. "Why — I — I — didn't know your name was Edgarton!" he managed finally to articulate.

An expression of ineffable triumph, and of triumph only, flickered in the Older Man's face.

"Why, that's just what I've been saying," he reiterated amiably. "You don't know anything!"

Fatuously the Younger Man rose to his feet, still struggling for speech — any old speech — a sentence, a word, a cough, anything, in fact, that would make a noise.

"Well, if little Miss Edgarton is — little Miss Edgarton," he babbled idiotically, "who in creation — are you?"

"Who am I?" stammered the Older Man perplexedly. As if the question really worried him, he sagged back a trifle against the sustaining wall of the house, and stood with his hands thrust deep in his pockets once more. "Who am I?" he repeated blandly. Again one eyebrow lifted. Again one side of his thin-lipped mouth twitched ever so slightly to the right. "Why, I'm just a man, Mr. Barton," he grinned very faintly, "who travels all over the world for the sake of whatever amusement he can get out of it. And some afternoons, of course, I get a good deal more amusement out of it — than I do others. Eh?"

Furiously the red blood mounted into the Young Man's cheeks. "Oh, I say, Edgarton!" he pleaded. Mirthlessly, wretchedly, a grin began to spread over his face. "Oh, I say!" he faltered. "I *am* a fool!"

The Older Man threw back his head and started to laugh.

At the first cackling syllable of the laugh, with appalling fatefulness Eve Edgarton herself loomed suddenly on the scene, in her old slouch hat, her gray flannel shirt, her weatherbeaten khaki Norfolk and riding-breeches, looking for all the world like an extraordinarily slim, extraordinarily shabby little boy just starting out to play. Up from the top of one riding-boot the butt of a revolver protruded slightly.

With her heavy black eyelashes shadowing somberly down across her olive-tinted cheeks, she passed Barton as if she did not even see him and went directly to her father.

"I am riding," she murmured almost inaudibly.

"In this heat?" groaned her father.

"In this heat," echoed Eve Edgarton.

"There will surely be a thunderstorm," protested her father.

"There will surely be a thunderstorm," acquiesced Eve Edgarton.

Without further parleying she turned and strolled off again.

Just for an instant the Older Man's glance followed her. Just for an instant with quizzically twisted eyebrows his glance flashed back sardonically to Barton's suffering face. Then very leisurely he began to laugh again.

But right in the middle of the laugh — as if something infinitely funnier than a joke had smitten him suddenly — he stopped short, with one eyebrow stranded halfway up his fore-head.

"Eve!" he called sharply. "Eve! Come back here a minute!"

Very laggingly from around the piazza corner the girl reappeared.

"Eve," said her father quite abruptly, "this is Mr. Barton! Mr. Barton, this is my daughter!"

Listlessly the girl came forward and proffered her hand to the Younger Man. It was a very little hand. More than that, it was an exceedingly cold little hand.

"How do you do, sir?" she murmured almost inaudibly.

With an expression of ineffable joy the Older Man reached out and tapped his daughter on the shoulder.

"It has just transpired, my dear Eve," he beamed, "that you can do this young man here an inestimable service — tell him something — teach him something, I mean — that he very specially needs to know!"

As one fairly teeming with benevolence he stood there smiling blandly into Barton's astonished face. "Next to the pleasure of bringing together two people who like each other," he persisted, "I know of nothing more poignantly diverting than the bringing together of people who — who —" Mockingly across his daughter's unconscious head, malevolently through his mask of utter guilelessness and peace, he challenged Barton's staring helplessness. "So — taken all in all," he drawled still beamingly, "there's nothing in the world — at this particular moment, Mr. Barton — that could amuse me more than to have you join my daughter in her ride this afternoon!"

"Ride with me?" gasped little Eve Edgarton.

"This afternoon?" floundered Barton.

"Oh — why — yes — of course! I'd be delighted! I'd be — be! Only — ! Only I'm afraid that — !"

Deprecatingly with uplifted hand the Older Man refuted every protest. "No, indeed, Mr. Barton," he insisted. "Oh, no — no indeed — I assure you it won't inconvenience my daughter in the slightest! My daughter is very obliging! My daughter, indeed — if I may say so in all modesty — my daughter indeed is always a good deal of a — philanthropist!"

Then very grandiloquently, like a man in an old-fashioned

picture, he began to back away from them, bowing low all the time, very, very low, first to Barton, then to his daughter, then to Barton again.

"I wish you both a very good afternoon!" he said. "Really, I see no reason why either of you should expect a single dull moment!"

Before the sickly grin on Barton's face his own smile deepened into actual unctuousness. But before the sudden woodeny set of his daughter's placid mouth his unctuousness twisted just a little bit wryly on his lips.

"After all, my dear young people," he asserted hurriedly, "there's just one thing in the world, you know, that makes two people congenial, and that is — that they both shall have arrived at exactly the same conclusion — by two totally different routes. It's got to be exactly the same conclusion, else there isn't any sympathy in it. But it's got to be by two totally different routes, you understand, else there isn't any talky-talk to it!"

Laboriously one eyebrow began to jerk its way up his forehead, and with a purely mechanical instinct he reached up drolly and pulled it down again. "So — as the initial test of your mutual congeniality this afternoon," he resumed, "I would therefore respectfully suggest as a special topic of conversation the consummate cheek of — yours truly, Paul Reymouth Edgarton!"

Starting to bow once more, he backed instead into the screen of the office window. Without even an expletive he turned, pushed in the screen, clambered adroitly through the aperture, and disappeared almost instantly from sight.

Very faintly from some far upstairs region the thin, faint, single syllable of a laugh came floating down into the piazza corner.

Then just as precipitous as a man steps into any other hole, Barton stepped into the conversational topic that had just been so aptly provided for him.

"Is your father something of a — of a practical joker, Miss Edgarton?" he demanded with the slightest possible tinge of shrillness.

For the first time in Barton's knowledge of little Eve Edgarton she lifted her eyes to him — great hazel eyes, great bored, dreary, hazel eyes set broadly in a too narrow olive face.

"My father is generally conceded to be something of a joker, I believe," she said dully. "But it would never have occurred to me to call him a particularly practical one. I don't like him," she added without a flicker of expression.

"I don't either!" snapped Barton.

A trifle uneasily little Eve Edgarton went on. "Why — once when I was a tiny child —" she droned.

"I don't know anything about when you were a tiny child," affirmed Barton with some vehemence. "But just this afternoon — !"

In striking contrast to the cool placidity of her face one of Eve Edgarton's boot-toes began to tap-tap-tap against the piazza floor. When she lifted her eyes again to Barton their sleepy sullenness was shot through suddenly with an unmistakable flash of temper.

"Oh, for Heaven's sake, Mr. Barton!" she cried out. "If you insist upon riding with me, couldn't you please hurry? The afternoons are so short!"

"If I 'insist' upon riding with you?" gasped Barton.

Disconcertingly from an upper window the Older Man's face beamed suddenly down upon him. "Oh, don't mind anything she says," drawled the Older Man. "It's just her cunning, 'meek' little ways."

Precipitately Barton bolted for his room.

Once safely ensconced behind his closed door a dozen different decisions, a dozen different indecisions, rioted tempestuously through his mind. To go was just as awkward as not to go! Not to go was just as awkward as to go! Over and over and over one silly alternative chased the other through his addled senses. Then just as precipitately as he had bolted to his room he began suddenly to hurl himself into his riding-clothes, yanking out a bureau drawer here, slamming back a closet door there, rummaging through a box, tipping over a trunk, yet in all his fuming haste, his raging irritability, showing the same fastidious choice of shirt, tie, collar, that characterized his every public appearance.

Immaculate at last as a tailor's equestrian advertisement he came striding down again into the hotel office, only to plunge most inopportunely into Miss Von Eaton's languorous presence.

"Why, Jim!" gasped Miss Von Eaton. Exquisitely white and cool and fluffy and dainty, she glanced up perplexedly at him from her lazy, deep-seated chair. "Why, Jim!" she repeated, just a little bit edgily. "Riding? Riding? Well, of all things! You who wouldn't even play bridge with us this afternoon on account of the heat! Well, who in the world — who can it be that has cut us all out?"

Teasingly she jumped up and walked to the door with him, and stood there peering out beyond the cool shadow of his dark-blue shoulder into the dazzling road where, like so many figures thrust forth all unwittingly into the merciless flare of a spotlight, little shabby Eve Edgarton and three sweating horses waited squintingly in the dust.

"Oh!" cried Miss Von Eaton. "W-why!" stammered Miss Von Eaton. "Good gracious!" giggled Miss Von Eaton. Then hysterically, with her hand clapped over her mouth, she turned and fled up the stairs to confide the absurd news to her mates.

With a face like a graven image Barton went on down the steps into the road. In one of his thirty-dollar riding-boots a disconcerting two-cent sort of squeak merely intensified his unhappy sensation of being motivated purely mechanically like a doll.

Two of the horses that whinnied cordially at his approach were rusty roans. The third was a chunky gray. Already on one of the roans Eve Edgarton sat perched with her bridle-rein oddly slashed in two, and knotted, each raw end to a stirrup, leaving her hands and arms still perfectly free to hug her mysterious books and papers to her breast.

"Good afternoon again, Miss Edgarton," smiled Barton conscientiously.

"Good afternoon again, Mr. Barton," echoed Eve Edgarton listlessly.

With frank curiosity he nodded toward her armful of papers. "Surely you're not going to carry — all that stuff with you?" he questioned.

"Yes, I am, Mr. Barton," drawled Eve Edgarton, scarcely above a whisper.

Worriedly he pointed to her stirrups. "But Great Scott, Miss Edgarton!" he protested. "Surely you're not reckless enough to ride like that? Just guiding with your feet?"

"I always — do, Mr. Barton," singsonged the girl monotonously.

"But the extra horse?" cried Barton. With a sudden little

chuckle of relief he pointed to the chunky gray. There was a side-saddle on the chunky gray. "Who's going with us?"

Almost insolently little Eve Edgarton narrowed her sleepy eyes.

"I always taken an extra horse with me, Mr. Barton — Thank you!" she yawned, with the very faintest possible tinge of asperity.

"Oh!" stammered Barton quite helplessly. "O-h-h!" Heavily, as he spoke, he lifted one foot to his stirrup and swung up into his saddle. Through all his mental misery, through all his physical discomfort, a single lovely thought sustained him. There was only one really good riding road in that vicinity! And it was shady! And, thank Heaven, it was most inordinately short!

But Eve Edgarton falsified the thought before he was half through thinking it.

She swung her horse around, reared him to almost a perpendicular height, merged herself like so much fluid khaki into his great, towering, threatening neck, reacted almost instantly to her own balance again, and went plunging off toward the wild, rough, untraveled foothills and — certain destruction, any unbiased onlooker would have been free to affirm!

Snortingly the chunky gray went tearing after her. A trifle sulkily Barton's roan took up the chase.

Shade? Oh, ye gods! If Eve Edgarton knew shade when she saw it she certainly gave no possible sign of such intelligence. Wherever the galloping, grass-grown road hesitated between green-roofed forest and devastated wood-lot, she chose the devastated wood-lot! Wherever the trotting, treacherous pasture faltered between hobbly, rock-strewn glare and soft, lush-carpeted spots of shade, she chose the hobbly, rock-strewn glare! On and on and on! Till dust turned sweat! And sweat turned dust again! On and on and on! With the riderless gray thudding madly after her! And Barton's sulky roan balking frenziedly at each new swerve and turn!

It must have been almost three miles before Barton quite overtook her. Then in the scudding, transitory shadow of a growly thundercloud she reined in suddenly, waited patiently till Barton's panting horse was nose and nose with hers, and then, pushing her slouch hat back from her low, curl-fringed forehead, jogged listlessly along beside him with her pale olive face turned inquiringly to his drenched, beet-colored visage.

"What was it that you wanted me to do for you, Mr. Barton?" she asked with a laborious sort of courtesy. "Are you writing a book or something that you wanted me to help you about? Is that it? Is that what Father meant?"

"Am I writing a — book?" gasped Barton. Desperately he began to mop his forehead. "Writing a book? Am — I — writing — a — book? Heaven forbid!"

"What are you doing?" persisted the girl bluntly.

"What am I doing?" repeated Barton. "Why, riding with you! Trying to ride with you!" he called out grimly as, taking the lead impetuously again, Eve Edgarton's horse shied off at a rabbit and went sidling down a sand-bank into a brand-new area of rocks and stubble and breast-high blueberry bushes.

Barton liked to ride and he rode fairly well, but he was by no means an equestrian acrobat, and, quite apart from the girl's unquestionably disconcerting mannerisms, the foolish floppity presence of the riderless gray rattled him more than he could possibly account for. Yet to save his life he could not have told which would seem more childish — to turn back in temper, or to follow on — in the same.

More in helplessness than anything else he decided to follow on.

"On and on and on," would have described it more adequately.

Blacker and blacker the huddling thundercaps spotted across the brilliant, sunny sky. Gaspier and gaspier in each lulling tree-top, in each hushing bird-song, in each drooping grass-blade, the whole torrid earth seemed to be sucking in its breath as if it meant never, never to exhale it again.

Once more in the midst of a particularly hideous glare the girl took occasion to rein in and wait for him, turning once more to his flushed, miserable countenance a little face inordinately pale and serene.

"If you're not writing a book, what would you like to talk about, Mr. Barton?" she asked conscientiously. "Would you like to talk about peat-bog fossils?"

"What?" gasped Barton.

"Peat-bog fossils," repeated the mild little voice. "Are you interested in peat-bog fossils? Or would you rather talk about the Mississippi River pearl fisheries? Or do you care more perhaps for politics? Would you like to discuss the relative financial conditions of the South American republics?"

Before the expression of blank despair in Barton's face, her own face fell a trifle. "No?" she ventured worriedly. "No? Oh, I'm sorry, Mr. Barton, but you see — you see — I've never been out before with anybody — my own age. So I don't know at all what you would be interested in!"

"Never been out before with any one her own age?" gasped Barton to himself. Merciful Heavens! what was her "own age"? There in her little khaki Norfolk and old slouch hat she looked about fifteen years old — and a boy, at that. Altogether wretchedly he turned and grinned at her.

"Miss Edgarton," he said, "believe me, there's not one thing today under God's heaven that does interest me — except the weather!"

"The weather?" mused little Eve Edgarton thoughtfully. Casually, as she spoke, she glanced down across the horses' lathered sides and up into Barton's crimson face. "The weather? Oh!" she hastened anxiously to affirm. "Oh, yes! The meteorological conditions certainly are interesting this summer. Do you yourself think that it's a shifting of the Gulf Stream? Or just a — just a change in the paths of the cyclonic areas of low pressure?" she persisted drearily.

"Eh?" gasped Barton. "The weather? Heat was what I meant, Miss Edgarton! Just plain heat! — *damned heat* — was what I meant — if I may be so explicit, Miss Edgarton."

"It is hot," conceded Eve apologetically.

"In fact," snapped Barton, "I think it's the hottest day I ever knew!"

"Really?" droned Eve Edgarton.

"Really!" snapped Barton.

It must have been almost half an hour before anybody spoke again. Then, "Pretty hot, isn't it?" Barton began all over again.

"Yes," said Eve Edgarton.

"In fact," hissed Barton through clenched teeth, "in fact I know it's the hottest day I ever knew!"

"Really?" droned Eve Edgarton.

"Really!" choked Barton.

Creakily under their hot, chafing saddles the sweltering roans lurched off suddenly through a great snarl of bushes into a fern-shaded spring-hole and stood ankle-deep in the boggy grass, guzzling noisily at food and drink, with the chunky gray crowding greedily against first one rider and then the other.

Quite against all intention Barton groaned aloud. His sun-scorched eyes seemed fairly shriveling with the glare. His wilted linen collar slopped like a stale poultice around his tortured neck. In his sticky fingers the bridle-rein itched like so much poisoned ribbon.

Reaching up one small hand to drag the soft flannel collar of her shirt a little farther down from her slim throat, Eve Edgarton rested her chin on her knuckles for an instant and surveyed him plaintively. "Aren't — we — having — an — awful time?" she whispered.

Even then if she had looked woman-y, girl-y, even remotely, affectedly feminine, Barton would doubtless have floundered heroically through some protesting lie. But to the frank, blunt, little-boyishness of her he succumbed suddenly with a beatific grin of relief. "Yes, we certainly are!" he acknowledged ruthlessly.

"And what good is it?" questioned the girl most unexpectedly.

"Not any good!" grunted Barton.

"To any one?" persisted the girl.

"Not to any one!" exploded Barton.

With an odd little gasp of joy the girl reached out dartingly and touched Barton on his sleeve. Her face was suddenly eager, active, transcendently vital.

"Then oh — won't you please — please — turn round — and go home — and leave me alone?" she pleaded astonishingly.

"Turn round and go home?" stammered Barton.

The touch on his sleeve quickened a little. "Oh, yes — please, Mr. Barton!" insisted the tremulous voice.

"You — you mean I'm in your way?" stammered Barton.

Very gravely the girl nodded her head. "Oh, yes, Mr. Barton — you're terribly in my way," she acknowledged quite frankly.

"Good Heavens," thought Barton, "is there a man in this? Is it a tryst? Well, of all things!"

Jerkily he began to back his horse out of the spring-hole,

back — back — back through the intricate, overgrown pathway of flapping leaves and sharp, scratchy twigs.

"I am very sorry, Miss Edgarton, to have forced my presence on you so!" he murmured ironically.

"Oh, it isn't just you!" said little Eve Edgarton quite frankly. "It's all Father's friends." Almost threateningly as she spoke she jerked up her own horse's drizzling mouth and rode right at Barton as if to force him back even faster through the great snarl of underbrush. "I hate clever people!" she asserted passionately. "I hate them — hate them — hate them! I hate all Father's clever friends! I hate —"

"But you see I'm not clever," grinned Barton in spite of himself. "Oh, not clever at all," he reiterated with some grimness as an alder branch slapped him stingingly across one eye. "Indeed —" he dodged and ducked and floundered, still backing, backing, everlastingly backing — "indeed, your father has spent quite a lot of his valuable time this afternoon assuring me — and reassuring me — that — that I'm altogether a fool!"

Unrelentingly little Eve Edgarton's horse kept right on forcing him back — back — back.

"But if you're not one of Father's clever friends — who are you?" she demanded perplexedly. "And why did you insist so on riding with me this afternoon?" she cried accusingly.

"I didn't exactly — insist," grinned Barton with a flush of guilt. The flush of guilt added to the flush of heat made him look suddenly very confused.

Across Eve Edgarton's thin little face the flash of temper faded instantly into mere sulky ennui again.

"Oh, dear — oh, dear," she droned. "You — you didn't want to marry me, did you?"

Just for one mad, panic-stricken second the whole world seemed to turn black before Barton's eyes. His heart stopped beating. His eardrums cracked. Then suddenly, astonishingly, he found himself grinning into that honest little face, and answering comfortably:

"Why, no, Miss Edgarton, I hadn't the slightest idea in the world of wanting to marry you."

"Thank God for that!" gasped little Eve Edgarton. "So many of Father's friends do want to marry me," she confided plaintively, still driving Barton back through that horrid scratchy thicket. "I'm so rich, you see," she confided with equal simplicity, "and I know so much — there's almost always somebody in Petrozavodsk or Broken Hill or Bashukulumbwe who wants to marry me."

"In — where?" stammered Barton.

"Why — in Russia!" said little Eve Edgarton with some surprise. "And Australia! And Africa! Were you never there?"

"I've been in Jersey City," babbled Barton with a desperate attempt at facetiousness.

"I was never there!" admitted little Eve Edgarton regretfully.

Vehemently with one hand she lunged forward and tried with her tiny open palm to push Barton's horse a trifle faster back through the intricate thicket. Then once in the open again she drew herself up with an absurd air of dignity and finality and bowed him from her presence.

"Good-by, Mr. Barton," she said. "Good-by, Mr. Barton."

"But Miss Edgarton —" stammered Barton perplexedly. Whatever his own personal joy and relief might be, the surrounding country nevertheless was exceedingly wild, and the girl an extravagantly long distance from home. "But Miss Edgarton —" he began all over again.

"Good-by, Mr. Barton! And thank you for going home!" she added conscientiously.

"But what will I tell your father?" worried Barton.

"Oh — hang Father," drawled the indifferent little voice.

"But the extra horse?" argued Barton with increasing perplexity. "The gray? If you've got some date up your sleeve, don't you want me to take the gray home with me, and get him out of your way?"

With sluggish resentment little Eve Edgarton lifted her eyes to his. "What would the gray go home with you for?" she asked tersely. "Why, how silly! Why, it's my — mother's horse! That is, we call it my mother's horse," she hastened to explain. "My mother's dead, you know. She's almost always been dead, I mean. So Father always makes me buy an extra place for my mother. It's just a trick of ours, a sort of a custom. I play around alone so much you know. And we live in such wild places!"

Casually she bent over and pushed the protruding butt of her revolver a trifle farther down into her riding boot. "S'long — Mr. Barton!" she called listlessly over the other, and started on, stumblingly, clatteringly, up the abruptly steep and precipitous mountain trail — a little dust-colored gnome on a dust-colored horse, with the dutiful gray pinking cautiously along behind her.

By some odd twist of his bridle-rein the gray's chunky neck arched slightly askew, and he pranced now and then from side to side of the trail as if guided thus by an invisible hand.

With an uncanny pucker along his spine as if he found himself suddenly deserting two women instead of one, Barton went fumbling and squinting out through the dusty green shade into the expected glare of the open pasture, and discovered, to his further disconcerting, that there was no glare left.

Before his astonished eyes he saw sun-scorched mountain-top, sun-scorched granite, sun-scorched field stubble turned suddenly to shade — no cool, translucent miracle of fluctuant greens, but a horrid, plushy, purple dusk under a horrid, plushy, purple sky, with a rip of lightning along the horizon, a galloping gasp of furiously oncoming wind, an almost strangling stench of dust-scented rain.

But before he could whirl his horse about, the storm broke! Heaven fell! Hell rose! The sides of the earth caved in! Chaos unspeakable tore north, east, south, west!

Snortingly for one single instant the roan's panic-stricken nostrils went blooming up into the cloudburst like two parched scarlet poinsettias. Then man and beast as one flesh, as one mind, went bolting back through the rain-drenched, wind-ravished thicket to find their mates.

Up, up, up, everlastingly up, the mountain trail twisted and scrambled through the unholy darkness. Now and again a slippery stone tripped the roan's fumbling feet. Now and again a swaying branch slapped Barton stingingly across his straining eyes. All around and about them tortured forest trees moaned and writhed in the gale. Through every cavernous vista gray sheets of rain went flapping madly by them. The lightning was incredible. The thunder like the snarl of a glass sky shivering into inestimable fragments.

With every gasping breath beginning to rip from his poor lungs like a knifed stitch, the roan still faltered on each new ledge to whinny desperately to his mate. Equally futilely from time to time, Barton, with his hands cupped to his mouth, holloed — holloed — holloed — into the thunderous darkness.

Then at a sharp turn in the trail, magically, in a pale, transient flicker of light, loomed little Eve Edgarton's boyish figure, drenched to the skin apparently, wind-driven, rain-battered, but with hands in her pockets, slouch hat rakishly askew, strolling as nonchalantly down that ghastly trail as a child might come strolling down a stained-glassed, Persian-carpeted stairway to meet an expected guest.

In vaguely silhouetted greeting for one fleet instant a little khaki arm lifted itself full length into the air.

Then more precipitately than any rational thing could happen, more precipitately than any rational thing could even begin to happen, could even begin to begin to happen, without shock, without noise, without pain, without terror or turmoil, or any time at all to fight or pray — a slice of living flame came scaling through the darkness — and cut Barton's consciousness clean in two!

CHAPTER II

When Barton recovered the severed parts of his consciousness again and tried to pull them together, he found that the Present was strangely missing.

The Past and the Future, however, were perfectly plain to him. He was a young stock-broker. He remembered that quite distinctly! And just as soon as the immediate dizzy mystery had been cleared up he would, of course, be a young stock-broker again! But between this snug conviction as to the Past, this smug assurance as to the Future, his mind lay tugging and shivering like a man under a split blanket. Where in creation was the Present? Alternately he tried to yank both Past and Future across the chilly interim.

"There was — a — green and white piazza corner," vaguely his memory reminded him. "Never again!" some latent determination leaped to mock him. And there had been — some sort of an argument — with a drollish old man — concerning all homely girls in general and one very specially homely little girl in particular. And the — very specially homely little girl in particular had turned out to be the old man's — daughter! — "Never again!" his original impulse hastened to reassure him. And there had been a horseback ride — with the girl. Oh, yes — out of some strained sense of — of parental humor — there had been a forced horseback ride. And the weather hadbeen — hot — and black — and then suddenly very yellow. Yellow? Yellow? Dizzily the world began to whir through his senses — a prism of light, a fume of sulphur! Yellow? Yellow? What was yellow? What was anything? What was anything? Yes! That was just it! Where was anything?

Whimperingly, like a dream-dazed dog, the soul of him began to shiver with fear. Oh, ye gods! If returning consciousness would only manifest itself first by some one indisputable proof of a still undisintegrated body, some crisp, reassuring method of outlining one's corporeal edges, some sensory roll-call, as it were of — head, hands, feet, sides! But out of oblivion, out of space abysmal, out of sensory annihilation, to come vaporing back, back, back, — headless, armless, legless, trunkless, conscious only of consciousness, uncertain yet whether the full awakening prove itself — this world or the next! As sacred of Heaven — as — of hell! As — !

Then very, very slowly, with no realization of eyelids, with no realization of lifting his eyelids, Barton began to see things. And he thought he was lying on the soft outer edges of a gigantic black pansy, staring blankly through its glowing golden center into the droll, sketchy little face of the pansy.

And then suddenly, with a jerk that seemed almost to crack his spine, he sensed that the blackness wasn't a pansy at all, but just a round, earthy sort of blackness in which he himself lay mysteriously prone. And he heard the wind still roaring furiously away off somewhere. And he heard the rain still drenching and sousing away off somewhere. But no wind seemed to be tugging directly at him, and no rain seemed to be splashing directly on him. And instead of the cavernous golden crater of a supernatural pansy there was just a perfectly tame yellow farm-lantern balanced adroitly on a low stone in the middle of the mysterious round blackness.

And in the sallow glow of that pleasant lantern-light little Eve Edgarton sat crosslegged on the ground with a great pulpy clutter of rain-soaked magazines spread out all around her like a giant's pack of cards. And diagonally across her breast from shoulder to waistline her little gray flannel shirt hung gashed into innumerable ribbons.

To Barton's blinking eyes she looked exceedingly strange and untidy. But nothing seemed to concern little Eve Edgarton except that spreading circle of half-drowned papers.

"For Heaven's sake — wha — ght are you — do'?" mumbled Barton.

Out from her flickering aura of yellow lantern-light little Eve Edgarton peered forth quizzically into Barton's darkness. "Why — I'm trying to save — my poor dear — books," she drawled.

"Wha — ght?" struggled Barton. The word dragged on his tongue like a weight of lead. "Wha — ght?" he persisted desperately. "Wh — ere? — For — Heaven's sake — wha — ght's the matter — with us?"

Solicitously little Eve Edgarton lifted a soggy magazine-page to the lantern's warm, curving cheek.

"Why — we're in my cave," she confided. "In my very own — cave — you know — that I was headed for — all the time. We got — sort of — struck by lightning," she started to explain. "We —"

"Struck by — lightning?" gasped Barton. Mentally he started to jump up. But physically nothing moved. "My God! I'm paralyzed!" he screamed.

"Oh, no — really — I don't think so," crooned little Eve Edgarton.

With the faintest possible tinge of reluctance she put down her papers, picked up the lantern, and, crawling over to where Barton lay, sat down cross-legged again on the ground beside him, and began with mechanically alternate fist and palm to rubadubdub and thump-thump-thump and stroke-stroke-stroke his utterly helpless body.

"Oh — of — course — you've had — an awfully close call!" she drummed resonantly upon his apathetic chest. "But I've seen — three lightning people — a lot worse off than you!" she kneaded reassuringly into his insensate neck-muscles. "And — they — came out of it — all right — after a few days!" she slapped mercilessly into his faintly conscious sides.

Very slowly, very sluggishly, as his circulation quickened again, a horrid suspicion began to stir in Barton's mind; but it took him a long time to voice the suspicion in anything as loud and public as words.

"Miss — Edgarton!" he plunged at last quite precipitately. "Miss Edgarton! Do I seem to have — any shirt on?"

"No, you don't seem to, exactly, Mr. Barton," conceded little Eve Edgarton. "And your skin —"

From head to foot Barton's whole body strained and twisted in a futile effort to raise himself to at least one elbow. "Why, I'm stripped to my waist!" he stammered in real horror.

"Why, yes — of course," drawled little Eve Edgarton. "And your skin —" Imperturbably as she spoke she pushed him down flat on the ground again and began, with her hands edged vertically like two slim boards, to slash little blissful gashes of consciousness and pain into his frigid right arm. "You see — I had to take both your shirts," she explained, "and what was left of your coat — and all of my coat — to make a soft, strong rope to tie round under your arms so the horse could drag you."

"Did the roan drag me — 'way up here?" groaned Barton a bit hazily.

With the faintest possible gasp of surprise little Eve Edgarton stopped slashing his arm and, picking up the lantern, flashed it disconcertingly across his blinking eyes and naked shoulders. "The roans are in heaven," she said quite simply. "It was Mother's horse that dragged you up here." As casually as if he had been a big doll she reached out one slim brown finger and drew his under lip a little bit down from his teeth. "My! But you're still blue!" she confided frankly. "I guess perhaps you'd better have a little more vodka."

Again Barton struggled vainly to raise himself on one elbow. "Vodka?" he stammered.

Again the lifted lantern light flashed disconcertingly across his face and shoulders. "Why, don't you remember — anything?" drawled little Eve Edgarton. "Not anything at all? Why, I must have worked over you two hours — artificial respiration, you know, and all that sort of thing — before I even got you up here! My! But you're heavy!" she reproached him frowningly. "Men ought to stay just as light as they possibly can, so when they get into trouble and things — it would be easier for women to help them. Why, last year in the China Sea — with Father and five of his friends — !"

A trifle shiveringly she shrugged her shoulders. "Oh, well, never mind about Father and the China Sea," she retracted soberly. "It's only that I'm so small, you see, and so flexible — I can crawl 'round most anywhere through port-holes and things — even if they're capsized. So we only lost one of them — one of Father's friends, I mean; and I never would have lost him if he hadn't been so heavy."

"Hours?" gasped Barton irrelevantly. With a wry twist of his neck he peered out through the darkness to where the freshening air, the steady, monotonous slosh-slosh-slosh of rain, the pale intermittent flare of stale lightning, proclaimed the opening of the cave.

"For Heaven's sake, what — what time is it?" he faltered.

"Why, I'm sure I don't know," said little Eve Edgarton. "But I should guess it might be about eight or nine o'clock. Are you hungry?"

With infinite agility she scrambled to her knees and went darting off on all fours like a squirrel into some mysterious, clattery corner of the darkness from which she emerged at last with one little gray flannel arm crooked inclusively around a whole elbowful of treasure.

"There," she drawled. "There. There. There."

Only the soft earthy thud that accompanied each "There" pointed the slightest significance to the word. The first thud was a slim, queer, stone flagon of vodka. Wanly, like some far pinnacle on some far Russian fortress, its grim shape loomed in the sallow lantern light. The second thud was a dust-colored basket of dates from some green-spotted Arabian desert. Vaguely its soft curving outline merged into shadow and turf. The third thud was a battered old drinking-cup — dully silver, mysteriously Chinese. The fourth thud was a big glass jar of frankly American beef. Familiarly, reassuringly, its sleek sides glinted in the flickering flame.

"Supper," announced little Eve Edgarton.

As tomboyishly as a miniature brigand she crawled forward again into the meager square of lantern-tinted earth and, yanking a revolver out of one boot and a pair of scissors from the other, settled herself with unassailable girlishness to jab the delicate scissors-points into the stubborn tin top of the meat jar.

As though the tin had been his own flesh the act goaded Barton half upright into the light — a brightly naked young Viking to the waist, a vaguely shadowed equestrian Fashion Plate to the feet.

"Well — I certainly never saw anybody like you before!" he glowered at her.

With equal gravity but infinitely more deliberation little Eve Edgarton returned the stare. "I never saw anybody like you before, either," she said enigmatically.

Barton winced back into the darkness. "Oh, I say," he stammered. "I wish I had a coat! I feel like a — like a —"

"Why — why?" droned little Eve Edgarton perplexedly. Out from the yellow heart of the pansy-blackness her small, grave, gnomish face peered after him with pristine frankness. "Why — why — I think you look — nice," said little Eve Edgarton.

With a really desperate effort Barton tried to clothe himself in facetiousness, if in nothing else. "Oh, very well," he grinned feebly. "If you don't mind — there's no special reason, I suppose, why I should."

Vaguely, blurrishly, like a figure on the wrong side of a stained-glass window, he began to loom up again into the lantern light. There was no embarrassment certainly about his hunger, nor any affectation at all connected with his thirst. Chokingly from the battered silver cup he gulped down the scorching vodka. Ravenously he attacked the salty meat, the sweet, cloying dates.

Watching him solemn-eyed above her own intermittent nibbles, the girl spoke out quite simply the thought that was uppermost in her mind. "This supper'll come in mighty handy, won't it, if we have to be out here all night, Mr. Barton?"

"If we have to be out here — all night?" faltered Barton.

Oh, ye gods! If just their afternoon ride together had been hotel talk — as of course it was within five minutes after their departure — what would their midnight return be? Or rather their non-return? Already through his addled brain he heard the monotonous creak-creak of rocking-chair gossip, the sly jest of the smoking-room, the whispered excitement of the kitchen — all the sophisticated old worldlings hoping indifferently for the best, all the unsophisticated old prudes yearning ecstatically for the worst!

"If we have to stay out here all night?" he repeated wildly. "Oh, what — oh, what will your father say, Miss Edgarton?"

"What will Father say?" drawled little Eve Edgarton. Thuddingly she set down the empty beef-jar. "Oh, Father'll say: What in creation is Eve out trying to save tonight? A dog? A cat? A three-legged deer?"

"Well, what do you expect to save?" quizzed Barton a bit tartly.

"Just — you," acknowledged little Eve Edgarton without enthusiasm. "And isn't it funny," she confided placidly, "that I've never yet succeeded in saving anything that I could take home with me — and keep! That's the trouble with boarding!"

In a vague, gold-colored flicker of appeal her lifted face flared out again into Barton's darkness. Too fugitive to be called a smile, a tremor of reminiscence went scudding across her mouth before the brooding shadow of her old slouch hat blotted out her features again.

"In India once," persisted the dreary little voice, "in India once, when Father and I were going into the mountains for the summer, there was a — there was a sort of fakir at one of the railway stations doing tricks with a crippled tiger-cub — a tiger-cub with a shot-off paw. And when Father wasn't looking I got off the train and went back — and I followed that fakir two days till he just naturally had to sell me the tiger-cub; he couldn't exactly have an Englishwoman following him indefinitely, you know. And I took the tiger-cub back with me to Father and he was very cunning — but —" Languorously the speech trailed off into indistinctness. "But the people at the hotel were — were indifferent to him," she rallied whisperingly. "And I had to let him go."

"You got off a train? In India? Alone?" snapped Barton. "And went following a dirty, sneaking fakir for two days? Well, of all the crazy — indiscreet —"

"Indiscreet?" mused little Eve Edgarton. Again out of the murky blackness her tilted chin caught up the flare of yellow lantern-light. "Indiscreet?" she repeated monotonously. "Who? I?"

"Yes — you," grunted Barton. "Traipsing 'round all alone — after —"

"But I never am alone, Mr. Barton," protested the mild little voice. "You see I always have the extra saddle, the extra railway ticket, the extra what-ever-it-is. And — and —" Caressingly a little gold-tipped hand reached out through the shadows and patted something indistinctly metallic. "My mother's memory? My father's revolver?" she drawled. "Why, what better company could any girl have? Indiscreet?" Slowly the tip of her little nose tilted up into the light. "Why, down in the Transvaal — two years ago," she explained painstakingly, "why, down in the Transvaal — two years ago — they called me the best-chaperoned girl in Africa. Indiscreet? Why, Mr. Barton, I never even saw an indiscreet woman in all my life. Men, of course, are indiscreet sometimes," she conceded conscientiously. "Down in the Transvaal two years ago, I had to shoot up a couple of men for being a little bit indiscreet, but —"

In one jerk Barton raised himself to a sitting posture.

"You 'shot up' a couple of men?" he demanded peremptorily.

Through the crook of a mud-smeared elbow shoving back the sodden brim of her hat, the girl glanced toward him like a vaguely perplexed little ragamuffin. "It was — messy," she admitted softly. Out from her snarl of storm-blown hair, tattered, battered by wind and rain, she peered up suddenly with her first frowning sign of self-consciousness. "If there's one thing in the world that I regret," she faltered deprecatingly, "it's a — it's — an untidy fight."

Altogether violently Barton burst out laughing. There was no mirth in the laugh, but just noise. "Oh, let's go home!" he suggested hysterically.

"Home?" faltered little Eve Edgarton. With a sluggish sort of defiance she reached out and gathered the big wet scrapbook to her breast. "Why, Mr. Barton," she said, "we couldn't get home now in all this storm and darkness and washout — to save our lives. But even if it were moonlight," she singsonged, "and starlight — and high-noon; even if there were — chariots — at the door, I'm not going home — now — till I've finished my scrapbook — if it takes a week."

"Eh?" jerked Barton. "What?" Laboriously he edged himself forward. For five hours now of reckless riding, of storm and privation, through death and disaster, the girl had clung tenaciously to her books and papers. What in creation was in them? "For Heaven's sake — Miss Edgarton —" he began.

"Oh, don't fuss — so," said little Eve Edgarton. "It's nothing but my paper-doll book."

"Your *paper-doll book*?" stammered Barton. With another racking effort he edged himself even farther forward. "Miss Edgarton!" he asked quite frankly, "are you — crazy?"

"N-o-o! But — very determined," drawled little Eve Edgarton. With unruffled serenity she picked up a pulpy magazine-page from the ground in front of her and handed it to him. "And it — would greatly facilitate matters, Mr. Barton," she confided, "if you would kindly begin drying out some papers against your side of the lantern."

"What?" gasped Barton.

Very gingerly he took the pulpy sheet between his thumb and forefinger. It was a full-page picture of a big gas-range, and slowly, as he scanned it for some hidden charm or value, it split in two and fell soggily back to its mates. Once again for sheer nervous relief he burst out laughing.

Out of her diminutiveness, out of her leanness, out of her extraordinary litheness, little Eve Edgarton stared up speculatively at Barton's great hulking helplessness. Her hat looked humorous. Her hair looked humorous. Her tattered flannel shirt was distinctly humorous. But there was nothing humorous about her set little mouth.

"If you — laugh," she threatened, "I'll tip you over backward again — and — trample on you."

"I believe you would!" said Barton with a sudden sobriety more packed with mirth than any laugh he had ever laughed.

"Well, I don't care," conceded the girl a bit sheepishly. "Everybody laughs at my paper-doll book! Father does! Everybody does! When I'm rearranging their old mummy collections — and cataloguing their old South American birds — or shining up their old geological specimens — they think I'm wonderful. But when I try to do the teeniest — tiniest thing that happens to interest me — they call me 'crazy'! So that's why I come 'way out here to this cave — to play," she whispered with a flicker of real shyness. "In all the world," she confided, "this cave is the only place I've ever found where there wasn't anybody to laugh at me."

Between her placid brows a vindictive little frown blackened suddenly. "That's why it wasn't specially convenient, Mr. Barton — to have you ride with me this afternoon," she affirmed. "That's why it wasn't specially convenient to — to have you struck by lightning this afternoon!" Tragically, with one small brown hand, she pointed toward the great water-soaked mess of magazines that surrounded her. "You see," she mourned, "I've been saving them up all summer — to cut out — today! And now? — Now — ? We're sailing for Melbourne Saturday!" she added conclusively.

"Well — really!" stammered Barton. "Well — truly! — Well, of all — damned things! Why — what do you want me to do? Apologize to you for having been struck by lightning?" His voice was fairly riotous with astonishment and indignation. Then quite unexpectedly one side of his mouth began to twist upward in the faintest perceptible sort of a real grin.

"When you smile like that you're — quite pleasant," murmured little Eve Edgarton.

"Is that so?" grinned Barton. "Well, it wouldn't hurt you to smile just a tiny bit now and then!"

"Wouldn't it?" said little Eve Edgarton. Thoughtfully for a moment, with her scissors poised high in the air, she seemed to be considering the suggestion. Then quite abruptly again she resumed her task of prying some pasted object out of her scrapbook. "Oh, no, thank you, Mr. Barton," she decided. "I'm much too bored — all the while — to do any smiling."

"Bored?" snapped Barton. Staring perplexedly into her dreary, meek little face, something deeper, something infinitely subtler than mere curiosity, wakened precipitately in his consciousness. "For Heaven's sake, Miss Edgarton!" he stammered. "From the Arctic Ocean to the South Seas, if you've seen all the things that you must have seen, if you've done all the things that you must have done — why should you look so bored?"

Flutteringly the girl's eyes lifted and fell. "Why, I'm bored, Mr. Barton," drawled little Eve Edgarton, "I'm bored because — I'm sick to death — of seeing all the things I've seen. I'm sick to death of — doing all the things I've done." With little metallic snips of sound she concentrated herself and her scissors suddenly upon the mahogany-colored picture of a pianola.

"Well, what do you want?" quizzed Barton.

In a sullen, turgid sort of defiance the girl lifted her somber eyes to his. "I want to stay home — like other people — and have a house," she wailed. "I want a house — and — the things that go with a house: a cat, and the things that go with a cat; kittens, and the things that go with kittens; saucers of cream, and the things that go with saucers of cream; ice-chests, and — and —" Surprisingly into her languid, singsong tone broke a sudden note of passion. "Bah!" she snapped. "Think of going all the way to India just to plunge your arms into the spooky, foamy Ganges and 'make a wish'! 'What do you wish?' asks Father, pleased as a Chessy-puss. Humph! I wish it was the soap suds in my own washtub! — Or gallivanting down to British Guiana just to smell the great blowsy waterlilies in the canals! I'd rather smell burned crackers in my own cook stove!"

"But you'll surely have a house — some time," argued Barton with real sympathy. Quite against all intention the girl's unexpected emotion disturbed him a little. "Every girl gets a house — some time!" he insisted resolutely.

"N-o-o, I don't — think so," mused Eve Edgarton judicially. "You see," she explained with soft, slow deliberation, "you see, Mr. Barton, only people who live in houses know people who live in houses! If you're a nomad you meet — only nomads! Campers mate just naturally with campers, and ocean travelers with ocean travelers — and red-velvet hotel-dwellers with red-velvet hotel-dwellers. Oh, of course, if Mother had lived it might have been different," she added a trifle more cheerfully. "For, of course, if Mother had lived I should have been — pretty," she asserted calmly, "or interesting-looking, anyway. Mother would surely have managed it — somehow; and I should have had a lot of beaux — young men beaux I mean, like you. Father's friends are all so gray! — Oh, of course, I shall marry — some time," she continued evenly. "Probably I'm going to marry the British consul at Nunko-Nono. He's a great friend of Father's — and he wants me to help him write a book on 'The Geologic Relationship of Melanesia to the Australian Continent'!"

Dully her voice rose to its monotone: "But I don't suppose — we shall live in a — house," she moaned apathetically. "At the best it will probably be only a musty room or two up over the consulate — and more likely than not it won't be anything at all except a nipa hut and a typewriter-table."

As if some mote of dust disturbed her, suddenly she rubbed the knuckles of one hand across her eyes. "But maybe we'll have — daughters," she persisted undauntedly. "And maybe they'll have houses!"

"Oh, shucks!" said Barton uneasily. "A — a house isn't so much!"

"It — isn't?" asked little Eve Edgarton incredulously. "Why — why — you don't mean —"

"Don't mean — what?" puzzled Barton.

"Do — you — live — in — a — house?" asked little Eve Edgarton abruptly. Her hands were suddenly quiet in her lap, her tousled head cocked ever so slightly to one side, her sluggish eyes incredibly dilated.

"Why, of course I live in a house," laughed Barton.

"O-h-h," breathed little Eve Edgarton. "Re — ally? It must be wonderful." Wiltingly her eyes, her hands, drooped back to her scrapbook again. "In — all — my — life," she resumed monotonously, "I've never spent a single night — in a real house."

"What?" questioned Barton.

"Oh, of course," explained the girl dully, "of course I've spent no end of nights in hotels and camps and huts and trains and steamers and — But — What color is your house?" she asked casually.

"Why, brown, I guess," said Barton.

"Brown, you 'guess'?" whispered the girl pitifully. "Don't you — know?"

"No, I wouldn't exactly like to swear to it," grinned Barton a bit sheepishly.

Again the girl's eyes lifted just a bit over-intently from the work in her lap.

"What color is the wallpaper — in your own room?" she asked casually. "Is it — is it a — dear pinkie-posie sort of effect? Or just plain — shaded stripes?"

"Why, I'm sure I don't remember," acknowledged Barton worriedly. "Why, it's just paper, you know — paper," he floundered helplessly. "Red, green, brown, white — maybe it's white," he asserted experimentally. "Oh, for goodness' sake — how should I know!" he collapsed at last. "When my sisters were home from Europe last year, they fixed the whole blooming place over for — some kind of a party. But I don't know that I ever specially noticed just what it was that they did to it. Oh, it's all right, you know!" he attested with some emphasis. "Oh, it's all right enough — early Jacobean, or something like that — 'perfectly corking,' everybody calls it! But it's so everlasting big, and it costs so much to run it, and I've lost such a wicked lot of money this year, that I'm not going to keep it after this autumn — if my sisters ever send me their Paris address so I'll know what to do with their things."

Frowningly little Eve Edgarton bent forward.

"'Some kind of a party?'" she repeated in unconscious mimicry. "You mean you gave a party? A real Christian party? As recently as last winter? And you can't even remember what kind of a party it was?" Something in her slender brown throat fluttered ever so slightly. "Why, I've never even been to a Christian party — in all my life!" she said. "Though I can dance in every language of Asia!

"And you've got sisters?" she stammered. "Live silk-and-muslin sisters? And you don't even know where they are? Why, I've never even had a girl friend in all my life!"

Incredulously she lifted her puzzled eyes to his. "And you've got a house?" she faltered. "And you're not going to keep it? A real — truly house? And you don't even know what color it is? You don't even know what color your own room is? And I know the name of every house-paint there is in the world," she muttered, "and the name of every wallpaper there is in the world, and the name of every carpet, and the name of every curtain, and the name of — everything. And I haven't got any house at all —"

Then startlingly, without the slightest warning, she pitched forward suddenly on her face and lay clutching into the turf — a little dust-colored wisp of a boyish figure sobbing its starved heart out against a dust-colored earth.

"Why — what's the matter!" gasped Barton. "Why! — Why — Kid!" Very laboriously with his numbed hands, with his strange, unresponsive legs, he edged himself forward a little till he could just reach her shoulder. "Why — Kid!" he patted her rather clumsily. "Why, Kid — do you mean —"

Slowly through the darkness Eve Edgarton came crawling to

his side. Solemnly she lifted her eyes to Barton's. "I'll tell you something that Mother told me," she murmured. "This is it: 'Your father is the most wonderful man that ever lived,' my mother whispered to me quite distinctly. 'But he'll never make any home for you — except in his arms; and that is plenty Home-Enough for a wife — but not nearly Home-Enough for a daughter! And — and —'"

"Why, you say it as if you knew it by heart," interrupted Barton.

"Why, of course I know it by heart!" cried little Eve Edgarton almost eagerly. "My mother whispered it to me, I tell you! The things that people shout at you — you forget in half a night. But the things that people whisper to you, you remember to your dying day!"

"If I whisper something to you," said Barton quite impulsively, "will you promise to remember it to your dying day?"

"Oh, yes, Mr. Barton," droned little Eve Edgarton.

Abruptly Barton reached out and tilted her chin up whitely toward him. "In this light," he whispered, "with your hat pushed back like — that! — and your hair fluffed up like — that! — and the little laugh in your eyes! — and the flush! — and the quiver! — you look like an — elf! A bronze and gold elf! You're wonderful! You're magical! You ought always to dress like that! Somebody ought to tell you about it! Woodsy, storm-colored clothes with little quick glints of light in them! Paquin or some of those people could make you famous!"

As spontaneously as he had touched her he jerked his hand away, and, snatching up the lantern, flashed it bluntly on her astonished face.

For one brief instant her hand went creeping up to the tip of her chin. Then very soberly, like a child with a lesson, she began to repeat Barton's impulsive phrases.

"'In this light,'" she droned, "'with your hat pushed back like that — and your hair fluffed up like that — and the — the —'" More unexpectedly then than anything that could possibly have happened she burst out laughing — a little low, giggly, schoolgirlish sort of laugh. "Oh, that's easy to remember!" she announced. Then, all one narrow black silhouette again, she crouched down into the semi-darkness.

"For a lady," she resumed listlessly, "who rode side-saddle and really enjoyed hiking 'round all over the sticky face of the globe, my mother certainly did guess pretty keenly just how things were going to be with me. I'll tell you what she said to sustain me," she repeated dreamily, "'Any foolish woman can keep house, but the woman who travels with your father has got to be able to keep the whole wide world for him! It's nations that you'll have to put to bed! And suns and moons and stars that you'll have to keep scoured and bright! But with the whole green earth for your carpet, and shining heaven for your roof-tree, and God Himself for your landlord, now wouldn't you be a fool, if you weren't quite satisfied?'"

"'If — you — weren't — quite satisfied,'" finished Barton mumblingly.

Little Eve Edgarton lifted her great eyes, soft with sorrow, sharp with tears, almost defiantly to Barton's.

"That's — what — Mother said," she faltered. "But all the same — I'd rather have a house!"

"Why, you poor kid!" said Barton. "You ought to have a house! It's a shame! It's a beastly shame! It's a —"

Very softly in the darkness his hand grazed hers.

"Did you touch my hand on purpose, or just accidentally?" asked Eve Edgarton, without a flicker of expression on her upturned, gold-colored face.

"Why, I'm sure I don't know," laughed Barton. "Maybe — maybe it was a little of each."

With absolute gravity little Eve Edgarton kept right on staring at him. "I don't know whether I should ever specially like you — or not, Mr. Barton," she drawled. "But you are certainly very beautiful!"

"Oh, I say!" cried Barton wretchedly. With a really desperate effort he struggled almost to his feet, tottered for an instant, and then came sagging down to the soft earth again — a great, sprawling, spineless heap, at little Eve Edgarton's feet.

Unflinchingly, as if her wrists were built of steel wires, the girl jumped up and pulled and tugged and yanked his almost dead weight into a sitting posture again.

"My! But you're chock-full of lightning!" she commiserated with him.

Out of the utter rage and mortification of his helplessness Barton could almost have cursed her for her sympathy. Then suddenly, without warning, a little gasp of sheer tenderness escaped him.

"Eve Edgarton," he stammered, "you're — a — brick! You — you must have been invented just for the sole purpose of saving people's lives. Oh, you've saved mine all right!" he acknowledged soberly. "And all this black, blasted night you've nursed me — and fed me — and jollied me — without a whimper about yourself — without — a —" Impulsively he reached out his numb-palmed hand to her, and her own hand came so cold to it that it might have been the caress of one ghost to another. "Eve Edgarton," he reiterated, "I tell you — you're a brick! And I'm a fool — and a slob — and a mutt-head — even when I'm not chock-full of lightning, as you call it! But if there's ever anything I can do for you!"

"What did you say?" muttered little Eve Edgarton.

"I said you were a brick!" repeated Barton a bit irritably.

"Oh, no, I didn't mean — that," mused the girl. "But what was the — last thing you said?"

"Oh!" grinned Barton more cheerfully. "I said — if there was ever anything that I could do for you, anything —"

"Would you rent me your attic?" asked little Eve Edgarton.

"Would I rent you my attic?" stammered Barton. "Why in the world should you want to hire my attic?"

"So I could buy pretty things in Siam — or Ceylon — or any other queer country — and have some place to send them," said little Eve Edgarton. "Oh, I'd pay the express, Mr. Barton," she hastened to assure him. "Oh, I promise you there never would be any trouble about the express! Or about the rent!" Expeditiously as she spoke she reached for her hip pocket and brought out a roll of bills that fairly took Barton's breath away. "If there's one thing in the world, you know, that I've got, it's money," she confided perfectly simply. "So you see, Mr. Barton," she added with sudden wistfulness, "there's almost nothing on the face of the globe that I couldn't have — if I only had some place to put it." Without further parleying she proffered the roll of bills to him.

"Miss Edgarton! Are you crazy?" Barton asked again quite precipitously.

Again the girl answered his question equally frankly, and

without offense. "Oh, no," she said. "Only very determined."

"Determined about what?" grinned Barton in spite of himself.

"Determined about an attic," drawled little Eve Edgarton.

With an unwonted touch of vivacity she threw out one hand in a little, sharp gesture of appeal; but not a tone of her voice either quickened or deepened.

"Why, Mr. Barton," she droned, "I'm thirty years old — and ever since I was born I've been traveling all over the world — in a steamer trunk. In a steamer trunk, mind you. With Father always standing over every packing to make sure that we never carry anything that — isn't necessary. With Father, I said," she re-emphasized by a sudden distinctness. "You know Father!" she added significantly.

"Yes — I know 'Father,'" assented Barton with astonishing glibness.

Once again the girl threw out her hand in an incongruous gesture of appeal.

"The things that Father thinks are necessary!" she exclaimed softly. Noiselessly as a shadow she edged herself forward into the light till she faced Barton almost squarely. "Maybe you think it's fun, Mr. Barton," she whispered. "Maybe you think it's fun — at thirty years of age — with all your faculties intact — to own nothing in the world except — except a steamer trunkful of the things that Father thinks are necessary!"

Very painstakingly on the fingers of one hand she began to enumerate the articles in question. "Just your riding togs," she said, "and six suits of underwear — and all the United States consular reports — and two or three wash dresses and two 'good enough' dresses — and a lot of quinine — and — a squashed hat — and — and —" Very faintly the ghost of a smile went flickering over her lips — "and whatever microscopes and specimen-cases get crowded out of Father's trunk. What's the use, Mr. Barton," she questioned, "of spending a whole year investigating the silk industry of China — if you can't take any of the silks home? What's the use, Mr. Barton, of rolling up your sleeves and working six months in a heathen porcelain factory — just to study glaze — if you don't own a china-closet in any city on the face of the earth? Why — sometimes, Mr. Barton," she confided, "it seems as if I'd die a horrible death if I couldn't buy things the way other people do — and send them somewhere — even if it wasn't 'home'! The world is so full of beautiful things," she mused. "White enamel bathtubs — and Persian rugs — and the most ingenious little eggbeaters — and —"

"Eh?" stammered Barton. Quite desperately he rummaged his brain for some sane-sounding expression of understanding and sympathy.

"You could, I suppose," he ventured, not too intelligently, "buy the things and give them to other people."

"Oh, yes, of course," conceded little Eve Edgarton without enthusiasm. "Oh, yes, of course, you can always buy people the things they want. But understand," she said, "there's very little satisfaction in buying the things you want to give to people who don't want them. I tried it once," she confided, "and it didn't work.

"The winter we were in Paraguay," she went on, "in some stale old English newspaper I saw an advertisement of a white bedroom set. There were eleven pieces, and it was adorable, and it cost eighty-two pounds — and I thought after I'd had the fun of unpacking it, I could give it to a woman I knew who had a tea plantation. But the instant she got it — she painted it — green! Now when you send to England for eleven pieces of furniture because they are white," sighed little Eve Edgarton, "and have them crated — because they're white — and sent to sea because they're white — and then carried overland — miles and miles and miles — on Indians' heads — because they're white, you sort of want 'em to stay white. Oh, of course it's all right," she acknowledged patiently. "The Tea Woman was nice, and the green paint by no means — altogether bad. Only, looking back now on our winter in Paraguay, I seem to have missed somehow the particular thrill that I paid eighty-two pounds and all that freightage for."

"Yes, of course," agreed Barton. He could see that.

"So if you could rent me your attic —" she resumed almost blithely.

"But my dear child," interrupted Barton, "what possible —"

"Why — I'd have a place then to send things to," argued little Eve Edgarton.

"But you're off on the high seas Saturday, you say," laughed Barton.

"Yes, I know," explained little Eve Edgarton just a bit impatiently. "But the high seas are so dull, Mr. Barton. And then we sail so long!" she complained. "And so far! — via this, via that, via every other stupid old port in the world! Why, it will be months and months before we ever reach Melbourne! And of course on every steamer," she began to monotone, "of course on every steamer there'll be some one with a mixed-up collection of shells or coins — and that will take all my mornings. And of course on every steamer there'll be somebody struggling with the Chinese alphabet or the Burmese accents — and that will take all my afternoons. But in the evenings when people are just having fun," she kindled again, "and nobody wants me for anything, why, then you see I could steal 'way up in the bow — where you're not allowed to go — and think about my beautiful attic. It's pretty lonesome," she whispered, "all snuggled up there alone with the night, and the spray and the sailors' shouts, if you haven't got anything at all to think about except just 'What's ahead? — What's ahead? — What's ahead?' And even that belongs to God," she sighed a bit ruefully.

With a quick jerk she edged herself even closer to Barton and sat staring up at him with her tousled head cocked on one side like an eager terrier.

"So if you just — could, Mr. Barton!" she began all over again. "And oh, I know it couldn't be any real bother to you!" she hastened to reassure him. "Because after Saturday, you know, I'll probably never — never be in America again!"

"Then what satisfaction," laughed Barton, "could you possibly get in filling up an attic with things that you will never see again?"

"What satisfaction?" repeated little Eve Edgarton perplexedly. "What satisfaction?" Between her placid brows a very black frown deepened. "Why, just the satisfaction," she said, "of knowing before you die, that you had definitely diverted to your own personality that much specific treasure out of the — out of the — world's chaotic maelstrom of generalities."

"Eh?" said Barton. "What? For Heaven's sake say it again!"

"Why — just the satisfaction —" began Eve Edgarton. Then abruptly the sullen lines grayed down again around her mouth.

"It seems funny to me, Mr. Barton," she almost whined, "that anybody as big as you are — shouldn't be able to understand anybody as little as — I am. But if I only had an attic!" she cried out with apparent irrelevance. "Oh, if just once in my whole life I could have even so much as an atticful of home! Oh, please — please — please, Mr. Barton!" she pleaded. "Oh, please!"

Precipitously she lifted her small brown face to his, and in her eyes he saw the strangest little unfinished expression flame up suddenly and go out again, a little fleeting expression so sweet, so shy, so transcendently lovely, that if it had ever lived to reach her frowning brow, her sulky little mouth, her — !

Then startlingly into his stare, into his amazement, broke a great white glare through the opening of the cave.

"My God!" he winced, with his elbow across his eyes.

"Why, it isn't lightning!" laughed little Eve Edgarton. "It's the moon!" Quick as a sprite she flashed to her feet and ran out into the moonlight. "We can go home now!" she called back triumphantly over her shoulder.

"Oh, we can, can we?" snapped Barton. His nerves were strangely raw. He struggled to his knees, and tottered there watching the cheeky little moonbeams lap up the mystery of the cave, and scare the yellow lantern-flame into a mere sallow glow.

Poignantly from the forest he heard Eve Edgarton's voice calling out into the night. "Come — Mother's — horse! Come — Mother's — horse H-o-o, hoo! Come — come — come!" Softly above the crackle of twigs, the thud of a hoof, the creak of a saddle, he sensed the long, tremulous, answering whinny. Then almost like a silver apparition the girl's figure and the horse's seemed to merge together before him in the moonlight.

"Well — of — all — things!" stammered Barton.

"Oh, the horse is all right. I thought he'd stay 'round," called the girl. "But he's wild as a hawk — and it's going to be the dickens of a job, I'm afraid, to get you up."

Half walking, half crawling, Barton emerged from the cave. "To get me up?" he scoffed. "Well, what do you think you're going to do?" Limply as he asked he sank back against the support of a tree.

"Why, I think," drawled Eve Edgarton, "I think — very naturally — that you're going to ride — and I'm going to walk — back to the hotel."

"Well, I am not!" snapped Barton. "Well, you are not!" he protested vehemently. "For Heaven's sake, Miss Edgarton, why don't you go scooting back on the gray and send a wagon or something for me?"

"Why, because it would make — such a fuss," droned little Eve Edgarton drearily. "Doors would bang — and lights would blaze — and somebody'd scream — and — and — you make so much fuss when you're born," she said, "and so much fuss when you die — don't you think it's sort of nice to keep things as quietly to yourself as you can all the rest of your days?"

"Yes, of course," acknowledged Barton. "But —"

"But nothing!" stamped little Eve Edgarton with sudden passion. "Oh, Mr. Barton — won't you please hurry! It's almost dawn now! And the nice hotel cook is very sick in a cot bed. And I promised her faithfully this noon that I'd make four hundred muffins for breakfast!"

"Oh, confound it!" said Barton.

Stumblingly he reached the big gray's side.

"But it's miles!" he protested in common decency. "Miles! — and miles! Rough walking, too, darned rough! And your poor little feet —"

"I don't walk particularly with my 'poor little feet,'" gibed Eve Edgarton. "Most especially, thank you, Mr. Barton, I walk with my big wanting-to-walk!"

"Oh," said Barton. "O-h-h." The bones in his knees began suddenly to slump like so many knots of tissue-paper. "Oh — all right — Eve!" he called out a bit hazily.

Then slowly and laboriously, with a very good imitation of meekness, he allowed himself to be pulled and pushed and jerked to the top of an old tree-stump, and from there at last, with many tricks and tugs and subterfuges, to the cramping side-saddle of the restive, rearing gray. Helplessly in the clear white moonlight he watched the girl's neck muscles cord and strain. Helplessly in the clear white moonlight he heard the girl's breath rip and tear like a dry sob out of her gasping lungs. And then at last, blinded with sweat, dizzy with weakness, as breathless as herself, as wrenched, as triumphant, he found himself clinging fast to a worn suede pommel, jogging jerkily down the mountainside with Eve Edgarton's doll-sized hand dragging hard on the big gray's curb and her whole tiny weight shoved back aslant and astrain against the big gray's too eager shoulder — little droll, colorless, "meek" Eve Edgarton, after her night of stress and terror, with her precious scrapbook still hugged tight under one arm striding stanchly home through the rough-footed, woodsy night to "make four hundred muffins for breakfast!"

At the first crook in the trail she glanced back hastily over her shoulder into the rustling shadows. "Good-by, Cave!" she called softly. "Good-by, Cave!" And once when some tiny woods-animal scuttled out from under her feet she smiled up a bit appealingly at Barton. Several times they stopped for water at some sudden noisy brook. And once, or twice, or even three times perhaps, when some blinding daze of dizziness overwhelmed him, she climbed up with one foot into the roomy stirrup and steadied his swaying, unfeeling body against her own little harsh, reassuring, flannel-shirted breast.

Mile after mile through the jet-black lattice-work of the tree-tops the August moon spotted brightly down on them. Mile after mile through rolling pastures the moon-plaited stubble crackled and sucked like a sheet of wet ice under their feet, then roads began — mere molten bogs of mud and moonlight; and little frail roadside bushes drunk with rain lay wallowing helplessly in every hollow.

Out of this pristine, uninhabited wilderness the hotel buildings loomed at last with startling conventionality. Even before their discreetly shuttered windows Barton winced back again with a sudden horrid new realization of his half-nakedness.

"For Heaven's sake!" he cried, "let's sneak in the back way somewhere! Oh Lordy! — what a sight I am to meet your father!"

"What a sight you are to — meet my father?" repeated Eve Edgarton with astonishment. "Oh, please don't insist on waking up Father," she begged. "He hates so to be waked up. Oh, of course if I'd been hurt it would have been courteous of you to tell him," she explained seriously. "But, oh, I'm sure he wouldn't like your waking him up just to tell him that you got hurt!"

Softly under her breath she began to whistle toward a shadow in the stable yard. "Usually," she whispered, "there's a sleepy stableboy lying round here somewhere. Oh — Bob!" she summoned.

Rollingly the shadow named "Bob" struggled to its very real feet.

"Here, Bob!" she ordered. "Come help Mr. Barton. He's pretty badly off. We got sort of struck by lightning. And two of us — got killed. Go help him upstairs. Do anything he wants. But don't make any fuss. He'll be all right in the morning."

Gravely she put out her hand to Barton, and nodded to the boy.

"Good night!" she said. "And good night, Bob!"

Shrewdly for a moment she stood watching them out of sight, shivered a little at the clatter of a box kicked over in some remote shed, and then swinging round quickly, ripped the hot saddle from the big gray's back, slipped the bit from his tortured tongue, and, turning him loose with one sharp slap on his gleaming flank, yanked off her own riding-boots and went scudding off in her stocking-feet through innumerable doors and else till, reaching the great empty office, she caromed off suddenly up three flights of stairs to her own apartment.

Once in her room her little traveling-clock told her it was a quarter of three.

"Whew!" she said. Just "Whew!" Very furiously at the big porcelain washbowl she began to splash and splash and splash. "If I've got to make four hundred muffins," she said, "I surely have got to be whiter than snow!"

Roused by the racket, her father came irritably and stood in the doorway.

"Oh, my dear Eve!" he complained, "didn't you get wet enough in the storm? And for mercy's sake where have you been?"

Out of the depths of her dripping hair and her big plushy bath-towel little Eve Edgarton considered her father only casually.

"Don't delay me!" she said, "I've got to make four hundred muffins! And I'm so late I haven't even time to change my clothes! We got struck by lightning," she added purely incidentally. "That is — sort of struck by lightning. That is, Mr. Barton got sort of struck by lightning. And oh, glory, Father!" her voice kindled a little. "And, oh, glory, Father, I thought he was gone! Twice in the hours I was working over him he stopped breathing altogether!"

Palpably the vigor died out of her voice again. "Father," she drawled mumblingly through intermittent flops of bath-towel; "Father — you said I could keep the next thing I — saved. Do you think I could — keep him?"

CHAPTER III

"What?" demanded her father.

Altogether unexpectedly little Eve Edgarton threw back her tousled head and burst out laughing.

"Oh, Father!" she jeered. "Can't you take a joke?"

"I don't know as you ever offered me one before," growled her father a bit ungraciously.

"All the same," asserted little Eve Edgarton with sudden seriousness — "all the same, Father, he did stop breathing twice. And I worked and I worked and I worked over him!" Slowly her great eyes widened.

"And oh, Father, his skin!" she whispered simply.

"Hush!" snapped her father with a great gust of resentment that he took to be a gust of propriety. "Hush, I say! I tell you it isn't delicate for a — for a girl to talk about a man's skin!"

"Oh — but his skin was very delicate," mused little Eve Edgarton persistently. "There in the lantern light —"

"What lantern light?" demanded her father.

"And the moonlight," murmured little Eve Edgarton.

"What moonlight?" demanded her father. A trifle quizzically he stepped forward and peered into his daughter's face. "Personally, Eve," he said, "I don't care for the young man. And I certainly don't wish to hear anything about his skin. Not anything! Do you understand? I'm very glad you saved his life," he hastened to affirm. "It was very commendable of you, I'm sure, and some one, doubtless, will be very much relieved. But for me personally the incident is closed! Closed, I said. Do you understand?"

Bruskly he turned back toward his own room, and then swung around again suddenly in the doorway.

"Eve," he frowned. "That was a joke — wasn't it? — what you said about wanting to keep that young man?"

"Why, of course!" said little Eve Edgarton.

"Well, I must say — it was an exceedingly clumsy one!"

growled her father irritably.

"Maybe so," droned little Eve Edgarton with unruffled serenity. "It was the first joke, you see, that I ever made." Slowly again her eyes began to widen. "All the same, Father," she said, "his —"

"Hush!" he ordered, and slammed the door conclusively behind him.

Very thoughtfully for a moment little Eve Edgarton kept right on standing there in the middle of the room. In her eyes was just the faintest possible suggestion of a smile. But there was no smile whatsoever about her lips. Her lips indeed were quite drawn and most flagrantly set with the expression of one who, having something determinate to say, will — yet — say it, somewhere, sometime, somehow, though the skies fall and all the waters of the earth dry up.

Then like the dart of a bird, she flashed to her father's door and opened it.

"Father!" she whispered. "Father!"

"Yes," answered the half-muffled, pillowy voice. "What is it?"

"Oh, I forgot to tell you something that happened once — down in Indo-China," whispered little Eve Edgarton. "Once when you were away," she confided breathlessly, "I pulled a half-drowned coolie out of a canal."

"Well, what of it?" asked her father a bit tartly.

"Oh, nothing special," said little Eve Edgarton, "except that his skin was like yellow parchment! And sandpaper! And old plaster!"

Without further ado then, she turned away, and, except for the single ecstatic episode of making the four hundred muffins for breakfast, resumed her pulseless role of being just — little Eve Edgarton.

As for Barton, the subsequent morning hours brought sleep and sleep only — the sort of sleep that fairly souses the senses in oblivion, weighing the limbs with lead, the brain with stupor, till the sleeper rolls out from under the load at last like one half paralyzed with cramp and helplessness.

Certainly it was long after noon-time before Barton actually rallied his aching bones, his dizzy head, his refractory inclinations, to meet the fluctuant sympathy and chaff that awaited him down-stairs in every nook and corner of the great, idle-minded hotel.

Conscientiously, but without enthusiasm, from the temporary retreat of the men's writing-room, he sent up his card at last to Mr. Edgarton, and was duly informed that that gentleman and his daughter were mountain-climbing. In an absurd flare of disappointment then, he edged his way out through the prattling piazza groups to the shouting tennis players, and on from the shouting tennis players to the teasing golfers, and back from the teasing golfers to the peaceful writing-room, where in a great, lazy chair by the open window he settled down once more with unwonted morbidness to brood over the grimly bizarre happenings of the previous night.

In a soft blur of sound and sense the names of other people came wafting to him from time to time, and once or twice at least the word "Barton" shrilled out at him with astonishing poignancy. Still like a man half drugged he dozed again — and woke in a vague, sweating terror — and dozed again — and dreamed again — and roused himself at last with the one violent determination to hook his slipping consciousness, whether or no, into the nearest conversation that he could reach.

The conversation going on at the moment just outside his window was not a particularly interesting one to hook one's attention into, but at least it was fairly distinct. In blissfully rational human voices two unknown men were discussing the non-domesticity of the modern woman. It was not an erudite discussion, but just a mere personal complaint.

"I had a house," wailed one, "the nicest, coziest house you ever saw. We were two years building it. And there was a garden — a real jim-dandy flower and vegetable garden — and there were twenty-seven fruit trees. But my wife —" the wail deepened — "my wife — she just would live in a hotel! Couldn't stand the 'strain,' she said, of 'planning food three times a day'! Not — 'couldn't stand the strain of earning meals three times a day' — you understand," the wailing voice added significantly, "but couldn't stand the strain of ordering 'em. People all around you, you know, starving to death for just — bread; but she couldn't stand the strain of having to decide between squab and tenderloin! Eh?"

"Oh, Lordy! You can't tell me anything!" snapped the other

voice more incisively. "Houses? I've had four! First it was the cellar my wife wanted to eliminate! Then it was the attic! Then it was — We're living in an apartment now!" he finished abruptly. "An apartment, mind you! One of those blankety — blank — blank — blank apartments!"

"Humph!" wailed the first voice again. "There's hardly a woman you meet these days who hasn't got rouge on her cheeks, but a man's got to go back — two generations, I guess, if he wants to find one that's got any flour on her nose!"

"Flour on her nose?" interrupted the sharper voice. "Flour on her nose? Oh, ye gods! I don't believe there's a woman in this whole hotel who'd know flour if she saw it! Women don't care any more, I tell you! They don't care!"

Just as a mere bit of physical stimulus the crescendoish stridency of the speech roused Barton to a lazy smile. Then, altogether unexpectedly, across indifference, across drowsiness, across absolute physical and mental non-concern, the idea behind the speech came hurtling to him and started him bolt upright in his chair.

"Ha!" he thought. "I know a girl that cares!" From head to foot a sudden warm sense of satisfaction glowed through him, a throb of pride, a puffiness of the chest. "Ha!" he gloated. "Ha —"

Then interruptingly from outside the window he heard the click of chairs hitching a bit nearer together.

"Sst!" whispered one voice. "Who's the freak in the 1830 clothes?"

"Why, that? Why, that's the little Edgarton girl," piped the other voice cautiously. "It isn't so much the '1830 clothes' as the 1830 expression that gets me! Where in creation —"

"Oh, upon my soul," groaned the man whose wife "would live in a hotel." "Oh, upon my soul — if there's one thing that I can't stand it's a woman who hasn't any style! If I had my way," he threatened with hissing emphasis, "if I had my way, I tell you, I'd have every homely looking woman in the world put out of her misery! Put out of my misery — is what I mean!"

"Ha! Ha! Ha!" chuckled the other voice.

"Ha! Ha! Ha!" gibed both voices ecstatically together.

With quite unnecessary haste Barton sprang to the window and looked out.

It was Eve Edgarton! And she did look funny! Not especially funny, but just plain, everyday little-Eve-Edgarton funny, in a shabby old English tramping suit, with a knapsack slung askew across one shoulder, a faded Alpine hat yanked down across her eyes, and one steel-wristed little hand dragging a mountain laurel bush almost as big as herself. Close behind her followed her father, equally shabby, his shapeless pockets fairly bulging with rocks, a battered tin botany kit in one hand, a dingy black camera-box in the other.

Impulsively Barton started out to meet them, but just a step from the threshold of the piazza door he sensed for the first time the long line of smokers watching the two figures grinningly above their puffy brown pipes and cigars.

"What is it?" called one smoker to another. "Moving Day in Jungle Town?"

"Ha! Ha! Ha!" tittered the whole line of smokers. "Ha! — Ha! Ha! Ha! — Ha!"

So, because he belonged, not so much to the type of person that can't stand having its friends laughed at, as to the type that can't stand having friends who are liable to be laughed at, Barton changed his mind quite precipitately about identifying himself at that particular moment with the Edgarton family, and whirled back instead to the writing-room. There, by the aid of the hotel clerk, and two bellboys, and three new blotters, and a different pen, and an entirely fresh bottle of ink, and just exactly the right-sized, the right-tinted sort of letter paper, he concocted a perfectly charming note to little Eve Edgarton — a note full of compliment, of gratitude, of sincere appreciation, a note reiterating even once more his persistent intention of rendering her somewhere, some-time, a really significant service!

Whereupon, thus duly relieved of his truly honest effort at self-expression, he went back again to his own kind — to the prat-tling, the well-groomed, the ultra-fashionables of both mind and body. And there on the shining tennis courts and the soft golf greens, through the late yellow afternoon and the first gray threat of twilight, the old sickening ennui came creeping back to his senses, warring chaotically there with the natural nervous reac-tion of his recent adventure, till just out of sheer morbid unrest, as soon as the flower-scented, candle-lighted dinner hour was over, he went stalking round and round the interminable piazzas, hunting in every dark corner for Mr. Edgarton and his daughter.

Meeting them abruptly at last in the full glare of the office, he clutched fatuously at Mr. Edgarton's reluctant attention with some quick question about the extraordinary moonlight, and stood by, grinning like any bashful schoolboy, while Mr. Edgarton explained to him severely, as if it were his fault, just why and to what extent the radii of mountain moonlight differed from the radii of any other kind of moonlight, and Eve herself, in absolute spiritual remoteness, stood patiently shifting her weight from one foot to the other, staring abstractedly all the time at the floor under her feet.

Right into the midst of this instructive discourse broke one of Barton's men friends with a sharp jog of his elbow, and a brief, apologetic nod to the Edgartons.

"Oh, I say, Barton!" cried the newcomer, breathlessly. "That wedding, you know, over across at the Kentons' tonight, with the Viennese orchestra — and Heaven knows what from New York? Well, we've shanghaied the whole business for a dance here tomorrow night! Music! Flowers! Palms! Catering! Everything! It's going to be the biggest little dancing party that this slice of North American scenery ever saw! And —"

Slowly little Eve Edgarton lifted her great solemn eyes to the newcomer's face.

"A party?" she drawled. "A — a — dancing party — you mean? A real — Christian — dancing party?"

Dully the big eyes drooped again, and as if in mere casual mannerism her little brown hands went creeping up to the white breast of her gown. Then just as startling, just as unprovable as the flash of a shooting star, her glance flashed up at Barton.

"O-h-h!" gasped little Eve Edgarton.

"O-h-h!" said Barton.

Astoundingly in his ears bells seemed suddenly to be ringing. His head was awhirl, his pulses fairly pounding with the weird, quixotic purport of his impulse.

"Miss Edgarton," he began. "Miss —"

Then right behind him two older men joggled him awkwardly in passing.

" — and that Miss Von Eaton," chuckled one man to another.

"Lordy! There'll be more than forty men after her for tomorrow night! Smith! Arnold! Hudson! Hazeltine! Who are you betting will get her?"

"I'm betting that i will!" crashed every brutally competitive male instinct in Barton's body. Impetuously he broke away from the Edgartons and darted off to find Miss Von Eaton before "Smith — Arnold — Hudson — Hazeltine" — or any other man should find her!

So he sent little Eve Edgarton a great, gorgeous box of candy instead, wonderful candy, pounds and pounds of it, fine, fluted chocolates, and rose-pink bonbons, and fat, sugared violets, and all sorts of tin-foiled mysteries of fruit and spice.

And when the night of the party came he strutted triumphantly to it with Helene Von Eaton, who already at twenty was beginning to be just a little bit bored with parties; and together through all that riot of music and flowers and rainbow colors and dazzling lights they trotted and tangoed with monotonous perfection — the envied and admired of all beholders; two superbly physical young specimens of manhood and womanhood, desperately condoning each other's dullnesses for the sake of each other's good looks.

And while Youth and its Laughter — a chaos of color and shrill crescendos — was surging back and forth across the flower-wreathed piazzas, and violins were wheedling, and Japanese lanterns drunk with candle light were bobbing gaily in the balsam-scented breeze, little Eve Edgarton, upstairs in her own room, was kneeling crampishly on the floor by the open window, with her chin on the windowsill, staring quizzically down — down — down on all that joy and novelty, till her father called her a trifle impatiently at last from his microscope table on the other side of the room.

"Eve!" summoned her father. "What an idler you are! Can't you see how worried I am over this specimen here? My eyes, I tell you, aren't what they used to be."

Then, patiently, little Eve Edgarton scrambled to her feet and, crossing over to her father's table, pushed his head mechanically aside and, bending down, squinted her own eye close to his magnifying glass.

"Bell-shaped calyx?" she began. "Five petals of the corollary partly united? Why, it must be some relation to the Mexican rain-tree," she mumbled without enthusiasm. "Leaves — alternate, bipinnate, very typically — few foliate," she continued. "Why, it's a — a Pithecolobium."

"Sure enough," said Edgarton. "That's what I thought all the time."

As one eminently relieved of all future worry in the matter, he jumped up, pushed away his microscopic work, and, grabbing up the biggest book on the table, bolted unceremoniously for an easy chair.

Indifferently for a moment little Eve Edgarton stood watching him. Then heavily, like a sleepy, insistent puppy dog, she shambled across the room and, climbing up into her father's lap, shoved aside her father's book, and burrowed her head triumphantly back into the lean, bony curve of his shoulder, her whole yawning interest centered apparently in the toes of her father's slippers.

Then so quietly that it scarcely seemed abrupt, "Father," she asked, "was my mother — beautiful?"

"What?" gasped Edgarton. "What?"

Bristling with a grave sort of astonishment he reached up nervously and stroked his daughter's hair. "Your mother," he winced. "Your mother was — to me — the most beautiful woman that ever lived! Such expression!" he glowed. "Such fire! But of such a spiritual modesty! Of such a physical delicacy! Like a rose," he mused, "like a rose — that should refuse to bloom for any but the hand that gathered it."

Languorously from some good practical pocket little Eve Edgarton extracted a much be-frilled chocolate bonbon and sat there munching it with extreme thoughtfulness. Then, "Father," she whispered, "I wish I was like — Mother."

"Why?" asked Edgarton, wincing.

"Because Mother's — dead," she answered simply.

Noisily, like an over conscious throat, the tiny traveling-clock on the mantelpiece began to swallow its moments. One moment — two moments — three — four — five — six moments — seven moments — on, on, on, gutturally, laboriously — thirteen — fourteen — fifteen — even twenty; with the girl still nibbling at her chocolate, and the man still staring off into space with that strange little whimper of pain between his pale, shrewd eyes.

It was the man who broke the silence first. Precipitately he shifted his knees and jostled his daughter to her feet.

"Eve," he said, "you're awfully spleeny tonight! I'm going to bed." And he stalked off into his own room, slamming the door behind him.

Once again from the middle of the floor little Eve Edgarton stood staring blankly after her father. Then she dawdled across the room and opened his door just wide enough to compass the corners of her mouth.

"Father," she whispered, "did Mother know that she was a rose — before you were clever enough to find her?"

"N-o," faltered her father's husky voice. "That was the miracle of it. She never even dreamed — that she was a rose — until I found her."

Very quietly little Eve Edgarton shut the door again and came back into the middle of her room and stood there hesitatingly for an instant.

Then quite abruptly she crossed to her bureau and pushing aside the old ivory toilet articles, began to jerk her tously hair first one way and then another across her worried forehead.

"But if you knew you were a rose?" she mused perplexedly to herself. "That is — if you felt almost sure that you were," she added with sudden humility. "That is —" she corrected herself — "that is — if you felt almost sure that you could be a rose — if anybody wanted you to be one?"

In impulsive experimentation she gave another tweak to her hair, and pinched a poor bruised-looking little blush into the hollow of one thin little cheek. "But suppose it was the — the people — going by," she faltered, "who never even dreamed that you were a rose? Suppose it was the — Suppose it was — Suppose —"

Dejection unspeakable settled suddenly upon her — an agonizing sense of youth's futility. Rackingly above the crash and lilt of music, the quick, wild thud of dancing feet, the sharp, staccato notes of laughter — she heard the dull, heavy, unrhythmical tread of the oncoming years — gray years, limping eternally from tomorrow on, through unloved lands, on unloved errands.

"This is the end of youth. It is — it is — it is," whimpered her heart.

"It *isn't!*" something suddenly poignant and determinate shrilled startlingly in her brain. "I'll have one more peep at youth, anyway!" threatened the brain.

"If we only could!" yearned the discouraged heart.

Speculatively for one brief instant the girl stood cocking her head toward the door of her father's room. Then, expeditiously, if not fashionably, she began at once to rearrange her tousled hair, and after one single pat to her gown — surely the quickest toilet-making of that festive evening — snatched up a slipper in each hand, crept safely past her father's door, crept safely out at last through her own door into the hall, and still carrying a slipper in each hand, had reached the head of the stairs before a new complexity assailed her.

"Why — why, I've never yet — been anywhere — alone — without my mother's memory!" she faltered, aghast.

Then impetuously, with a little frown of material inconvenience, but no flicker whatsoever in the fixed spiritual habit of her life, she dropped her slippers on the floor, sped back to her room, hesitated on the threshold a moment with real perplexity, darted softly to her trunk, rummaged as noiselessly through it as a kitten's paws, discovered at last the special object of her quest — a filmy square of old linen and lace — thrust it into her belt with her own handkerchief, and went creeping back again to her slippers at the head of the stairs.

As if to add fresh nervousness to the situation, one of the slippers lay pointing quite boldly downstairs. But the other slipper — true as a compass to the north — toed with unmistakable severity toward the bedroom.

Tentatively little Eve Edgarton inserted one foot in the timid slipper. The path back to her room was certainly the simplest path that she knew — and the dullest. Equally tentatively she withdrew from the timid slipper and tried the adventurous one. "O-u-c-h!" she cried out loud. The sole of the second slipper seemed fairly sizzling with excitement.

With a slight gasp of impatience, then, she reached out and pulled the timid slipper back into line, stepped firmly into it, pointed both slipper-toes unswervingly southward, and proceeded on downstairs to investigate the "Christian Dance."

At the first turn of the lower landing she stopped short, with every ennui-darkened sense in her body "jacked" like a wild deer's senses before the sudden dazzle of sight, sound, scent that awaited her below. Before her blinking eyes she saw even the empty, humdrum hotel office turned into a blazing bower of palms and roses and electric lights. Beyond this bower a corridor opened out — more dense, more sweet, more sparkling. And across this corridor the echo of the unseen ball came diffusing through the palms — the plaintive cry of a violin, the rippling laugh of a piano, the swarming hum of human voices, the swish of skirts, the agitant thud-thud-thud of dancing feet, the throb, almost, of young hearts — a thousand commonplace, everyday sounds merged here and now into one magic harmony that thrilled little Eve Edgarton as nothing on God's big earth had ever thrilled her before.

Hurriedly she darted down the last flight of steps and sped across the bright office to the dark veranda, consumed by one fuming, passionate, utterly uncontrollable curiosity to see with her own eyes just what all that wonderful sound looked like!

Once outside in the darkness her confusion cleared a little. It was late, she reasoned — very, very late, long after midnight probably; for of all the shadowy, flickering line of evening smokers that usually crowded that particular stretch of veranda only a single distant glow or two remained. Yet even now in the almost complete isolation of her surroundings the old inherent bashfulness swept over her again and warred chaotically with her insistent purpose. As stealthily as possible she crept along the dark wall to the one bright spot that flared forth like a lantern lens from the gay ballroom — crept along — crept along — a plain little girl in a plain little dress, yearning like all the other plain little girls of the world, in all the other plain little dresses of the world, to press her wistful little nose just once against some dazzling toy-shop window.

With her fingers groping at last into the actual shutters of that coveted ballroom window, she scrunched her eyes up perfectly tight for an instant and then opened them, staring wide at the entrancing scene before her.

"Oh!" said little Eve Edgarton. "Oh!"

The scene was certainly the scene of a most madcap summer

carnival. Palms of the far December desert were there! And roses from the near, familiar August gardens! The swirl of chiffon and lace and silk was like a rainbow-tinted breeze! The music crashed on the senses like blows that wasted no breath in subtler argument! Naked shoulders gleamed at every turn beneath their diamonds! Silk stockings bared their sheen at each new rompish step! And through the dizzy mystery of it all — the haze, the maze, the vague, audacious unreality, — grimly conventional, blatantly tangible white shirt-fronts surrounded by great black blots of men went slapping by — each with its share of fairyland in its arms!

"Why! They're not dancing!" gasped little Eve Edgarton. "They're just prancing!"

Even so, her own feet began to prance. And very faintly across her cheekbones a little flicker of pink began to glow.

Then very startlingly behind her a man's shadow darkened suddenly, and, sensing instantly that this newcomer also was interested in the view through the window, she drew aside courteously to give him his share of the pleasure. In her briefest glance she saw that he was no one whom she knew, but in the throbbing witchery of the moment he seemed to her suddenly like her only friend in the world.

"It's pretty, isn't it?" she nodded toward the ballroom.

Casually the man bent down to look until his smoke-scented cheek almost grazed hers. "It certainly is!" he conceded amiably.

Without further speech for a moment they both stood there peering into the wonderful picture. Then altogether abruptly, and with no excuse whatsoever, little Eve Edgarton's heart gave a great, big lurch, and, wringing her small brown hands together so that by no grave mischance should she reach out and touch the stranger's sleeve as she peered up at him, "I — can dance," drawled little Eve Edgarton.

Shrewdly the man's glance flashed down at her. Quite plainly he recognized her now. She was that "funny little Edgarton girl." That's exactly who she was! In the simple, old-fashioned arrangement of her hair, in the personal neatness but total indifference to fashion of her prim, high-throated gown, she represented — frankly — everything that he thought he most approved in woman. But nothing under the starry heavens at that moment could have forced him to lead her as a partner into that dazzling maelstrom of Mode and Modernity, because she looked "so horridly eccentric and conspicuous" — compared to the girls that he thought he didn't approve of at all!

"Why, of course you can dance! I only wish I could!" he lied gallantly. And stole away as soon as he reasonably could to find another partner, trusting devoutly that the darkness had not divulged his actual features.

Five minutes later, through the windowframe of her magic picture, little Eve Edgarton saw him pass, swinging his share of fairyland in his arms.

And close behind him followed Barton, swinging his share of fairyland in his arms! Barton the wonderful — at his best! Barton the wonderful — with his best, the blonde, blonde girl of the marvelous gowns and hats. There was absolutely no doubt whatsoever about them. They were the handsomest couple in the room!

Furtively from her hidden corner little Eve Edgarton stood and watched them. To her appraising eyes there were at least two other girls almost as beautiful as Barton's partner. But no other man in the room compared with Barton. Of that she was perfectly sure! His brow, his eyes, his chin, the way he held his head upon his wonderful shoulders, the way he stood upon his feet, his smile, his laugh, the very gesture of his hands!

Over and over again as she watched, these two perfect partners came circling through her vision, solemnly graceful or rhythmically hoydenish — two fortune-favored youngsters born into exactly the same sphere, trained to do exactly the same things in exactly the same way, so that even now, with twelve years' difference in age between them, every conscious vibration of their beings seemed to be tuned instinctively to the same key.

Bluntly little Eve Edgarton looked back upon the odd, haphazard training of her own life. Was there any one in this world whose training had been exactly like hers? Then suddenly her elbow went crooking up across her eyes to remember how Barton had looked in the stormy woods that night — lying half naked — and almost wholly dead — at her feet. Except for her odd, haphazard training, he would have been dead! Barton, the beautiful — dead? And worse than dead — buried? And worse than —

Out of her lips a little gasp of sound rang agonizingly.

And in that instant, by some trick-fashion of the dance, the rollicking music stopped right off short in the middle of a note, the lights went out, the dancers fled precipitously to their seats, and out of the arbored gallery of the orchestra a single swarthy-faced male singer stepped forth into the wan wake of an artificial moon, and lifted up a marvelous tenor voice in one of those weird folk-songs of the faraway that fairly tear the listener's heart out of his body — a song as sinisterly metallic as the hum of hate along a dagger-blade; a song as rapturously surprised at its own divinity as the first trill of a nightingale; a song of purling brooks and grim, gray mountain fortresses; a song of quick, sharp lights and long, low, lazy cadences; a song of love and hate; a song of all joys and all sorrows — and then death; the song of Sex as Nature sings it — the plaintive, wheedling, passionate song of Sex as Nature sings it yet — in the faraway places of the earth.

To no one else in that company probably did a single word penetrate. Merely stricken dumb by the vibrant power of the voice, vaguely uneasy, vaguely saddened, group after group of hoydenish youngsters huddled in speechless fascination around the dark edges of the hall.

But to little Eve Edgarton's cosmopolitan ears each familiar gipsyish word thus strangely transplanted into that alien room was like a call to the wild — from the wild.

So — as to all repressed natures the moment of full self-expression comes once, without warning, without preparation, without even conscious acquiescence sometimes — the moment came to little Eve Edgarton. Impishly first, more as a dare to herself than as anything else, she began to hum the melody and sway her body softly to and fro to the rhythm.

Then suddenly her breath began to quicken, and as one half hypnotized she went clambering through the window into the ballroom, stood for an instant like a gray-white phantom in the outer shadows, then, with a laugh as foreign to her own ears as to another's, snatched up a great, square, shimmering silver scarf that gleamed across a deserted chair, stretched it taut by its corners across her hair and eyes, and with a queer little cry — half defiance, half appeal — a quick dart, a long, undulating glide — merged herself into the dagger-blade, the nightingale, the grim mountain fortress, the gay mocking brook, all the love, all the rapture, all the ghastly fatalism of that heartbreaking song.

Bent as a bow her lithe figure curved now right, now left, to the lilting cadence. Supple as a silken tube her slender body seemed to drink up the fluid sound. No one could have sworn in that vague light that her feet even so much as touched the ground. She was a wraith! A phantasy! A fluctuant miracle of sound and sense!

Tremulously the singer's voice faltered in his throat to watch his song come gray-ghost-true before his staring eyes. With scant restraint the crowd along the walls pressed forward, half pleasure-mad, to solve the mystery of the apparition. Abruptly the song stopped! The dancer faltered! Lights blazed! A veritable shriek of applause went roaring to the rooftops!

And little Eve Edgarton in one wild panic-stricken surge of terror went tearing off through a blind alley of palms, dodging a cafe table, jumping an improvised trellis — a hundred pursuing voices yelling: "Where is she? Where is she?" — the telltale tinsel scarf flapping frenziedly behind her, flapping — flapping — till at last, between one high, garnished shelf and another it twined its vampirish chiffon around the delicate fronds of a huge potted fern! There was a jerk, — a blur, — a blow, the sickening crash of fallen pottery — And little Eve Edgarton crumpled up on the floor, no longer "colorless" among the pale, dry, rainbow tints and shrill metallic glints of that most wondrous scene.

Under her crimson mask, when the rescuers finally reached her, she lay as perfectly disguised as even her most bashful mood could have wished.

All around her — kneeling, crowding, meddling, interfering — frightened people queried: "Who is she? Who is she?" Now and again from out of the medley some one offered a half-articulate suggestion. It was the hotel proprietor who moved first. Clumsily but kindly, with a fat hand thrust under her shoulders, he tried to raise her head from the floor. Barton himself, as the most recently returned from the "Dark Valley," moved next. Futilely, with a tiny wisp of linen and lace that he found at the girl's belt, he tried to wipe the blood from her lips.

"Who is she? Who is she?" the conglomerate hum of inquiry rose and fell like a moan.

Beneath the crimson stain on the little lace handkerchief a

trace of indelible ink showed faintly. Scowlingly Barton bent to decipher it. "Mother's Little Handkerchief," the marking read. "'Mother's?'" Barton repeated blankly. Then suddenly full comprehension broke upon him, and, horridly startled and shocked with a brand-new realization of the tragedy, he fairly blurted out his astonishing information.

"Why — why, it's the — little Edgarton girl!" he hurled like a bombshell into the surrounding company.

Instantly, with the mystery once removed, a dozen hysterical people seemed startled into normal activity. No one knew exactly what to do, but some ran for water and towels, and some ran for the doctor, and one young woman with astonishing acumen slipped out of her white silk petticoat and bound it, blue ribbons and all, as best she could, around Eve Edgarton's poor little gashed head.

"We must carry her upstairs!" asserted the hotel proprietor.

"I'll carry her!" said Barton quite definitely.

Fantastically the procession started upward — little Eve Edgarton white as a ghost now in Barton's arms, except for that one persistent trickle of red from under the loosening edge of her huge Orientallike turban of ribbon and petticoat; the hotel proprietor still worrying eternally how to explain everything; two or three well-intentioned women babbling inconsequently of other broken heads.

In astonishingly slow response to as violent a knock as they thought they gave, Eve Edgarton's father came shuffling at last to the door to greet them. Like one half paralyzed with sleep and perplexity, he stood staring blankly at them as they filed into his rooms with their burden.

"Your daughter seems to have bumped her head!" the hotel proprietor began with professional tact.

In one gasping breath the women started to explain their version of the accident.

Barton, as dumb as the father, carried the girl directly to the bed and put her down softly, half lying, half sitting, among the great pile of night-crumpled pillows. Some one threw a blanket over her. And above the top edge of that blanket nothing of her showed except the grotesquely twisted turban, the whole of one white eyelid, the half of the other, and just that single persistent trickle of red. Raspishly at that moment the clock on the mantel-piece choked out the hour of three. Already Dawn was more than half a hint in the sky, and in the ghastly mixture of real and artificial light the girl's doom looked already sealed.

Then very suddenly she opened her eyes and stared around.

"Eve!" gasped her father, "what have you been doing?"

Vaguely the troubled eyes closed, and then opened again. "I was — trying — to show people — that I was a — rose," mumbled little Eve Edgarton.

Swiftly her father came running to her side. He thought it was her deathbed statement. "But Eve?" he pleaded. "Why, my own little girl. Why, my —"

Laboriously the big eyes lifted to his. "Mother was a rose," persisted the stricken lips desperately.

"Yes, I know," sobbed her father. "But — but —"

"But — nothing," mumbled little Eve Edgarton. With an almost superhuman effort she pushed her sharp little chin across the confining edge of the blanket. Vaguely, unrecognizingly then, for the first time, her heavy eyes sensed the hotel proprietor's presence and worried their way across the tearful ladies to Barton's harrowed face.

"Mother — was a rose," she began all over again. "Mother — was a rose. Mother — was — a rose," she persisted babblingly. "And Father — g-guessed it — from the very first! But as for me — ?" Weakly she began to claw at her incongruous bandage. "But — as — for me," she gasped, "the way I'm fixed! — I have to — announce it!"

CHAPTER IV

The Edgartons did not start for Melbourne the following day! Nor the next — nor the next — nor even the next.

In a head-bandage much more scientific than a blue-ribboned petticoat, but infinitely less decorative, little Eve Edgarton lay imprisoned among her hotel pillows.

Twice a day, and oftener if he could justify it, the village doctor came to investigate pulse and temperature. Never before in all his humdrum winter experience, or occasional summer-tourist vagary, had he ever met any people who prated of camels instead of motorcars, or deprecated the dust of Abyssinia on their Piccadilly shoes, or sighed indiscriminately for the snow-tinted breezes of the Klondike and Ceylon. Never, either, in all his full round of experience had the village doctor had a surgical patient as serenely complacent as little Eve Edgarton, or any anxious relative as madly restive as little Eve Edgarton's father.

For the first twenty-four hours, of course, Mr. Edgarton was much too worried over the accident to his daughter to think for a moment of the accident to his railway and steamship tickets. For the second twenty-four hours he was very naturally so much concerned with the readjustment of his railway and steamship tickets that he never concerned himself at all with the accident to his plans. But by the end of the third twenty-four hours, with his first two worries reasonably eliminated, it was the accident to his plans that smote upon him with the fiercest poignancy. Let a man's clothes and togs vacillate as they will between his trunk and his bureau — once that man's spirit is packed for a journey nothing but journey's end can ever unpack it again!

With his own heart tuned already to the heartthrob of an engine, his pale eyes focused squintingly toward expected novelties, his thin nostrils half-a-sniff with the first salty scent of the Far-Away, Mr. Edgarton, whatever his intentions, was not the most ideal of sickroom companions. Too conscientious to leave his daughter, too unhappy to stay with her, he spent the larger part of his days and nights pacing up and down like a caged beast between the two bedrooms.

It was not till the fifth day, however, that his impatience actually burst the bounds he had set for it. Somewhere between his maple bureau and Eve's mahogany bed the actual explosion took place, and in that explosion every single infinitesimal wrinkle of brow, cheek, chin, nose, was called into play, as if here at last was a man who intended once and for all time to wring his face perfectly dry of all human expression.

"Eve!" hissed her father. "I hate this place! I loathe this place! I abominate it! I despise it! The flora is — execrable! The fauna? Nil! And as to the coffee — the breakfast coffee? Oh, ye gods! Eve, if we're delayed here another week — I shall die! Die, mind you, at sixty-two! With my life-work just begun, Eve! I hate this place! I abominate it! I de — ”

"Really?" mused little Eve Edgarton from her white pillows. "Why — I think it's lovely."

"Eh?" demanded her father. "What? Eh?"

"It's so social," said little Eve Edgarton.

"Social?" choked her father.

As bereft of expression as if robbed of both inner and outer vision, little Eve Edgarton lifted her eyes to his. "Why — two of the hotel ladies have almost been to see me," she confided listlessly. "And the chambermaid brought me the picture of her beau. And the hotel proprietor lent me a storybook. And Mr. —"

"Social?" snapped her father.

"Oh, of course — if you got killed in a fire or anything, saving people's lives, you'd sort of expect them to — send you candy — or make you some sort of a memorial," conceded little Eve Edgarton unemotionally. "But when you break your head — just amusing yourself? Why, I thought it was nice for the hotel ladies to almost come to see me," she finished, without even so much as a flicker of the eyelids.

Disgustedly her father started for his own room, then whirled abruptly in his tracks and glanced back at that imperturbable little figure in the big white bed. Except for the scarcely perceptible houndlike flicker of his nostrils, his own face held not a whit more expression than the girl's.

"Eve," he asked casually, "Eve, you're not changing your mind, are you, about Nunko-Nono? And John Ellbertson? Good old John Ellbertson," he repeated feelingly. "Eve!" he quickened with sudden sharpness. "Surely nothing has happened to make you change your mind about Nunko-Nono? And good old John Ellbertson?"

"Oh — no — Father," said little Eve Edgarton. Indolently she withdrew her eyes from her father's and stared off Nunko-Nono-ward — in a hazy, geographical sort of a dream. "Good old John Ellbertson — good old John Ellbertson," she began to croon very softly to herself. "Good old John Ellbertson. How I do love his kind brown eyes — how I do —"

"Brown eyes?" snapped her father. "Brown? John Ellbertson's got the grayest eyes that I ever saw in my life!"

Without the slightest ruffle of composure little Eve Edgarton accepted the correction. "Oh, has he?" she conceded amiably. "Well, then, good old John Ellbertson — good old John Ellbertson — how I do love his kind — gray eyes," she began all over again.

Palpably Edgarton shifted his standing weight from one foot to the other. "I understood — your mother," he asserted a bit defiantly.

"Did you, dear? I wonder?" mused little Eve Edgarton.

"Eh?" jerked her father.

Still with the vague geographical dream in her eyes, little Eve Edgarton pointed off suddenly toward the open lid of her steamer trunk.

"Oh — my manuscript notes, Father, please!" she ordered almost peremptorily, "John's notes, you know? I might as well be working on them while I'm lying here."

Obediently from the tousled top of the steamer trunk her father returned with the great batch of rough manuscript. "And my pencil, please," persisted little Eve Edgarton. "And my eraser. And my writing-board. And my ruler. And my —"

Absent-mindedly, one by one, Edgarton handed the articles to her, and then sank down on the foot of her bed with his thin-lipped mouth contorted into a rather mirthless grin. "Don't care much for your old father, do you?" he asked trenchantly.

Gravely for a moment the girl sat studying her father's weather-beaten features, the thin hair, the pale, shrewd eyes, the gaunt cheeks, the indomitable old-young mouth. Then a little shy smile flickered across her face and was gone again.

"As a parent, dear," she drawled, "I love you to distraction! But as a daily companion?" Vaguely her eyebrows lifted. "As a real playmate?" Against the starch-white of her pillows the sudden flutter of her small brown throat showed with almost startling distinctness. "But as a real playmate," she persisted evenly, "you are so — intelligent — and you travel so fast — it tires me."

"Whom do you like?" asked her father sharply.

The girl's eyes were suddenly sullen again — bored, distrait, inestimably dreary. "That's the whole trouble," she said. "You've never given me time — to like anybody."

"Oh, but — Eve," pleaded her father. Awkward as any schoolboy, he sat there, fuming and twisting before this absurd little bunch of nerve and nerves that he himself had begotten. "Oh, but Eve," he deprecated helplessly, "it's the deuce of a job for a — for a man to be left all alone in the world with a — with a daughter! Really it is!"

Already the sweat had started on his forehead, and across one cheek the old gray fretwork of wrinkles began to shadow suddenly. "I've done my best!" he pleaded. "I swear I have! Only I've never known how! With a mother, now," he stammered, "with a wife, with a sister, with your best friend's sister, you know just what to do! It's a definite relation! Prescribed by a definite emotion! But a daughter? Oh, ye gods! Your whole sexual angle of vision changed! A creature neither fish, flesh, nor fowl! Nonsuperior, non-contemporaneous, non-subservient! Just a lady! A strange lady! Yes, that's exactly it, Eve — a strange lady — growing eternally just a little bit more strange — just a little bit more remote — every minute of her life! Yet it's so — damned intimate all the time!" he blurted out passionately. "All the time she's rowing you about your manners and your morals, all the time she's laying down the law to you about the tariff or the turnips, you're remembering — how you used to — scrub her — in her first little blue-lined tin bathtub!"

Once again the flickering smile flared up in little Eve Edgarton's eyes and was gone again. A trifle self-consciously she burrowed back into her pillows. When she spoke her voice was scarcely audible. "Oh, I know I'm funny," she admitted conscientiously.

"You're not funny!" snapped her father.

"Yes, I am," whispered the girl.

"No, you're not!" reasserted her father with increasing vehemence. "You're not! It's I who am funny! It's I who —" In a chaos of emotion he slid along the edge of the bed and clasped her in his arms. Just for an instant his wet cheek grazed hers, then: "All the same, you know," he insisted awkwardly, "I hate this place!"

Surprisingly little Eve Edgarton reached up and kissed him full on the mouth. They were both very much embarrassed.

"Why — why, Eve!" stammered her father. "Why, my little — little girl! Why, you haven't kissed me — before — since you were a baby!"

"Yes, I have!" nodded little Eve Edgarton.

"No, you haven't!" snapped her father.

"Yes, I have!" insisted Eve.

Tighter and tighter their arms clasped round each other. "You're all I've got," faltered the man brokenly.

"You're all I've ever had," whispered little Eve Edgarton.

Silently for a moment each according to his thoughts sat staring off into far places. Then without any warning whatsoever, the man reached out suddenly and tipped his daughter's face up abruptly into the light.

"Eve!" he demanded. "Surely you're not blaming me any in your heart because I want to see you safely married and settled with — with John Ellbertson?"

Vaguely, like a child repeating a dimly understood lesson, little Eve Edgarton repeated the phrases after him. "Oh, no, Father," she said, "I surely am not blaming you — in my heart — for wanting to see me married and settled with — John Ellbertson. Good old John Ellbertson," she corrected painstakingly.

With his hand still holding her little chin like a vise, the man's eyes narrowed to his further probing. "Eve," he frowned, "I'm not as well as I used to be! I've got pains in my arms! And they're not good pains! I shall live to be a thousand! But I — I might not! It's a — rotten world, Eve," he brooded, "and quite unnecessarily crowded — it seems to me — with essentially rotten people. Toward the starving and the crippled and the hideously distorted, the world, having no envy of them, shows always an amazing mercy; and Beauty, whatever its sorrows, can always retreat to the thick protecting wall of its own conceit. But as for the rest of us?" he grinned with a sudden convulsive twist of the eyebrow, "God help the unduly prosperous — and the merely plain! From the former — always, Envy, like a wolf, shall tear down every fresh talent, every fresh treasure, they lift to their aching backs. And from the latter — Brutal Neglect shall ravage away even the charm that they thought they had!

"It's a — a rotten world, Eve, I tell you," he began all over again, a bit plaintively. "A rotten world! And the pains in my arms, I tell you, are not — nice! Distinctly not nice! Sometimes, Eve, you think I'm making faces at you! But, believe me, it isn't faces that I'm making! It's my — heart that I'm making at you! And believe me, the pain is not — nice!"

Before the sudden wince in his daughter's eyes he reverted instantly to an air of semi-jocosity. "So, under all existing circumstances, little girl," he hastened to affirm, "you can hardly blame a crusty old codger of a father for preferring to leave his daughter in the hands of a man whom he positively knows to be good, than in the hands of some casual stranger who, just in a negative way, he merely can't prove isn't good? Oh, Eve — Eve," he pleaded sharply, "you'll be so much better off — out of the world! You've got infinitely too much money and infinitely too little — self-conceit — to be happy here! They would break your heart in a year! But at Nunko-Nono!" he cried eagerly. "Oh, Eve! Think of the peace of it! Just white beach, and a blue sea, and the long, low, endless horizon. And John will make you a garden! And women — I have often heard — are very happy in a garden! And —"

Slowly little Eve Edgarton lifted her eyes again to his. "Has John got a beard?" she asked.

"Why — why, I'm sure I don't remember," stammered her father. "Why, yes, I think so — why, yes, indeed — I dare say!"

"Is it a grayish beard?" asked little Eve Edgarton.

"Why — why, yes — I shouldn't wonder," admitted her father.

"And reddish?" persisted little Eve Edgarton. "And longish? As long as — ?" Illustratively with her hands she stretched to her full arm's length.

"Yes, I think perhaps it is reddish," conceded her father. "But why?"

"Oh — nothing," mused little Eve Edgarton. "Only sometimes at night I dream about you and me landing at Nunko-Nono. And John in a great big, long, reddish-gray beard always comes crunching down at full speed across the hermit-crabs to meet us. And always just before he reaches us, he — he trips on his beard — and falls headlong into the ocean — and is — drowned."

"Why — what an awful dream!" deprecated her father.

"Awful?" queried little Eve Edgarton. "Ha! It makes me — laugh. All the same," she affirmed definitely, "good old John Ellbertson will have to have his beard cut." Quizzically for an instant she stared off into space, then quite abruptly she gave a quick, funny little sniff. "Anyway, I'll have a garden, won't I?" she said. "And always, of course, there will be — Henrietta."

"Henrietta?" frowned her father.

"My daughter!" explained little Eve Edgarton with dignity.

"Your daughter?" snapped Edgarton.

"Oh, of course there may be several," conceded little Eve Edgarton. "But Henrietta, I'm almost positive, will be the best one!"

So jerkily she thrust her slender throat forward with the speech, her whole facial expression seemed suddenly to have undercut and stunned her father's.

"Always, Father," she attested grimly, "with your horrid old books and specimens you have crowded my dolls out of my steamer trunk. But never once —" her tightening lips hastened to assure him, "have you ever succeeded in crowding — Henrietta — and the others out of my mind!"

Quite incongruously, then, with a soft little hand in which there lurked no animosity whatsoever, she reached up suddenly and smoothed the astonishment out of her father's mouth-lines.

"After all, Father," she asked, "now that we're really talking so intimately, after all — there isn't so specially much to life anyway, is there, except just the satisfaction of making the complete round of human experience — once for yourself — and then once again — to show another person? Just that double chance, Father, of getting two original glimpses at happiness? One through your own eyes, and one — just a little bit dimmer — through the eyes of another?"

With mercilessly appraising vision the starving Youth that was in her glared up at the satiate Age in him.

"You've had your complete round of human experience, Father!" she cried. "Your first — full — untrammeled glimpse of all your Heart's Desires. More of a glimpse, perhaps, than most people get. From your tiniest boyhood, Father, everything just as you wanted it! Just the tutors you chose in just the subjects you chose! Everything then that American colleges could give you! Everything later that European universities could offer you! And then Travel! And more Travel! And more! And more! And then — Love! And then Fame! 'Love, Fame, and Far Lands!' Yes, that's it exactly! Everything just as you chose it! So your only tragedy, Father, lies — as far as I can see — in just little — me! Because I don't happen to like the things that you like, the things that you already have had the first full joy of liking, — you've got to miss altogether your dimmer, secondhand glimpse of happiness! Oh, I'm sorry, Father! Truly I am! Already I sense the hurt of these latter years — the shattered expectations, the incessant disappointments! You who have stared unblinkingly into the face of the sun, robbed in your twilight of even a candle-flame. But, Father?"

Grimly, despairingly, but with unfaltering persistence — Youth fighting with its last gasp for the rights of its Youth — she lifted her haggard little face to his. "But, Father! — my tragedy lies in the fact — that at thirty — I've never yet had even my first-hand glimpse of happiness! And now apparently, unless I'm willing to relinquish all hope of ever having it, and consent to 'settle down,' as you call it, with 'good old John Ellbertson' — I'll never even get a gamble — probably — at sighting Happiness second-hand through another person's eyes!"

"Oh, but Eve!" protested her father. Nervously he jumped up and began to pace the room. One side of his face was quite grotesquely distorted, and his lean fingers, thrust precipitously into his pockets, were digging frenziedly into their own palms. "Oh, but Eve!" he reiterated sharply, "you will be happy with John! I know you will! John is a — John is a — Underneath all that slowness, that ponderous slowness — that — that — Underneath that —"

"That longish — reddish — grayish beard?" interpolated little Eve Edgarton.

Glaringly for an instant the old eyes and the young eyes challenged each other, and then the dark eyes retreated suddenly before — not the strength but the weakness of their opponents.

"Oh, very well, Father," assented little Eve Edgarton. "Only —" ruggedly the soft little chin thrust itself forth into stubborn outline again. "Only, Father," she articulated with inordinate distinctness, "you might just as well understand here and now, I won't budge one inch toward Nunko-Nono — not one single solitary little inch toward Nunko-Nono — unless at London, or Lisbon, or Odessa, or somewhere, you let me fill up all the trunks I want to — with just plain pretties — to take to Nunko-Nono! It isn't exactly, you know, like a bride moving fifty miles out from town somewhere," she explained painstakingly. "When a bride goes out to a place like Nunko-Nono, it isn't enough, you understand, that she takes just the things she needs. What she's got to take, you see, is everything under the sun — that she ever may need!"

With a little soft sigh of finality she sank back into her pillows, and then struggled up for one brief instant again to add a postscript, as it were, to her ultimatum. "If my day is over — without ever having been begun," she said, "why, it's over — without ever having been begun! And that's all there is to it! But when it comes to Henrietta," she mused, "Henrietta's going to have five-inch hair-ribbons — and everything else — from the very start!"

"Eh?" frowned Edgarton, and started for the door.

"And oh, Father!" called Eve, just as his hand touched the doorknob. "There's something I want to ask you for Henrietta's sake. It's rather a delicate question, but after I'm married I suppose I shall have to save all my delicate questions to — ask John; and John, somehow, has never seemed to me particularly canny about anything except — geology. Father!" she asked, "just what is it — that you consider so particularly obnoxious in — in — young men? Is it their sins?"

"Sins!" jerked her father. "Bah! It's their traits!"

"So?" questioned little Eve Edgarton from her pillows. "So? Such as — what?"

"Such as the pursuit of woman!" snapped her father. "The love — not of woman, but of the pursuit of woman! On all sides you see it today! On all sides you hear it — sense it — suffer it! The young man's eternally jocose sexual appraisement of woman! 'Is she young? Is she pretty?' And always, eternally, 'Is there any one younger? Is there any one prettier?' Sins, you ask?" Suddenly now he seemed perfectly willing, even anxious, to linger and talk. "A sin is nothing, oftener than not, but a mere accidental, non-considered act! A yellow streak quite as exterior as the scorch of a sunbeam. And there is no sin existent that a man may not repent of! And there is no honest repentance, Eve, that a wise woman cannot make over into a basic foundation for happiness! But a trait? A congenital tendency? A yellow streak bred in the bone? Why, Eve! If a man loves, I tell you, not woman, but the pursuit of woman? So that — wherever he wins — he wastes again? So that indeed at last, he wins only to waste? Moving eternally — on —

on — on from one ravaged lure to another? Eve! Would I deliver over you — your mother's reincarnated body — to — to such as that?"

"O-h-h," said little Eve Edgarton. Her eyes were quite wide with horror. "How careful I shall have to be with Henrietta."

"Eh?" snapped her father.

Ting-a-ling — ling — ling — ling! trilled the telephone from the farther side of the room.

Impatiently Edgarton came back and lifted the receiver from its hook. "Hello?" he growled. "Who? What? Eh?"

With quite unnecessary vehemence he rammed the palm of his hand against the mouthpiece and glared back over his shoulder at his daughter. "It's that — that Barton!" he said. "The impudence of him! He wants to know if you are receiving visitors today! He wants to know if he can come up! The —"

"Yes — isn't it — awful?" stammered little Eve Edgarton.

Imperiously her father turned back to the telephone. Ting-a-ling — ling — ling — ling, chirped the bell right in his face. As if he were fairly trying to bite the transmitter, he thrust his lips and teeth into the mouthpiece.

"My daughter," he enunciated with extreme distinctness, "is feeling quite exhausted — exhausted — this afternoon. We appreciate, of course Mr. Barton, your — What? Hello there!" he interrupted himself sharply. "Mr. Barton? Barton? Now what in the deuce?" he called back appealingly toward the bed. "Why, he's rung off! The fool!" Quite accidentally then his glance lighted on his daughter. "Why, what are you smoothing your hair for?" he called out accusingly.

"Oh, just to put it on," acknowledged little Eve Edgarton.

"But what in creation are you putting on your coat for?" he demanded tartly.

"Oh, just to smooth it," acknowledged little Eve Edgarton.

With a sniff of disgust Edgarton turned on his heel and strode off into his own room.

For five minutes by the little traveling-clock, she heard him pacing monotonously up and down — up and down. Then very softly at last she summoned him back to her.

"Father," she whispered, "I think there's some one knocking at the outside door."

"What?" called Edgarton. Incredulously he came back through his daughter's room and, crossing over to the hall door, yanked it open abruptly on the intruder.

"Why — good afternoon!" grinned Barton above the extravagantly large and languorous bunch of pale lavender orchids that he clutched in his hand.

"Good afternoon!" said Edgarton without enthusiasm.

"Er — orchids!" persisted Barton still grinningly. Across the unfriendly hunch of the older man's shoulder he caught a disquieting glimpse of a girl's unduly speculative eyes. In sudden impulsive league with her against this, their apparent common enemy, Age, he thrust the orchids into the older man's astonished hands.

"For me?" questioned Edgarton icily.

"Why, yes — certainly!" beamed Barton. "Orchids, you know! Hothouse orchids!" he explained painstakingly.

"So I — judged," admitted Edgarton. With extreme distaste he began to untie the soft flimsy lavender ribbon that encompassed them. "In their native state, you know," he confided, "one very seldom finds them growing with — sashes on them." From her nest of cushions across the room little Eve Edgarton loomed up suddenly into definite prominence.

"What did you bring me, Mr. Barton?" she asked.

"Why, Eve!" cried her father. "Why, Eve, you astonish me! Why, I'm surprised at you! Why — what do you mean?"

The girl sagged back into her cushions. "Oh, Father," she faltered, "don't you know — anything? That was just 'small talk.'"

With perfunctory courtesy Edgarton turned to young Barton. "Pray be seated," he said; "take — take a chair."

It was the chair closest to little Eve Edgarton that Barton took. "How do you do, Miss Edgarton?" he ventured.

"How do you do, Mr. Barton?" said little Eve Edgarton.

From the splashy wash-stand somewhere beyond them, they heard Edgarton fussing with the orchids and mumbling vague Latin imprecations — or endearments — over them. A trifle surreptitiously Barton smiled at Eve. A trifle surreptitiously Eve smiled back at Barton.

In this perfectly amiable exchange of smiles the girl reached up suddenly to the sides of her head. "Is my — is my bandage on straight?" she asked worriedly.

"Why, no," admitted Barton; "it ought not to be, ought it?"

Again for no special reason whatsoever they both smiled.

"Oh, I say," stammered Barton. "How you can dance!"

Across the girl's olive cheeks her heavy eyelashes shadowed down like a fringe of black ferns. "Yes — how I can dance," she murmured almost inaudibly.

"Why didn't you let anybody know?" demanded Barton.

"Yes — why didn't I let anybody know?" repeated the girl in an utter panic of bashfulness.

"Oh, I say," whispered Barton, "won't you even look at me?"

Mechanically the girl opened her eyes and stared at him fixedly until his own eyes fell.

"Eve!" called her father sharply from the next room, "where in creation is my data concerning North American orchids?"

"In my steamer-trunk," began the girl. "On the left hand side. Tucked in between your riding-boots and my best hat."

"O-h-h," called her father.

Barton edged forward in his chair and touched the girl's brown, boyish little hand.

"Really, Miss Eve," he stammered, "I'm awfully sorry you got hurt! Truly I am! Truly it made me feel awfully squeamish! Really I've been thinking a lot about you these last few days! Honestly I have! Never in all my life did I ever carry any one as little and hurt as you were! It sort of haunts me, I tell you. Isn't there something I could do for you?"

"Something you could do for me?" said little Eve Edgarton, staring. Then again the heavy lashes came shadowing down across her cheeks.

"I haven't had any very great luck," she said, "in finding you ready to do things for me."

"What?" gasped Barton.

The big eyes lifted and fell again. "There was the attic," she whispered a bit huskily. "You wouldn't rent me your attic!"

"Oh, but — I say!" grinned Barton. "Some real thing, I mean! Couldn't I — couldn't I — read aloud to you?" he articulated quite distinctly, as Edgarton came rustling back into the room with his arms full of papers.

"Read aloud?" gibed Edgarton across the top of his spectacles. "It's a daring man, in this unexpurgated day and generation, who offers to read aloud to a lady."

"He might read me my geology notes," suggested little Eve Edgarton blandly.

"Your geology notes?" hooted her father. "What's this? Some more of your new-fangled 'small talk'? Your geology notes?" Still chuckling mirthlessly, he strode over to the big table by the window and, spreading out his orchid data over every conceivable inch of space, settled himself down serenely to compare one "flower of mystery" with another.

Furtively for a moment Barton sat studying the gaunt, graceful figure. Then quite impulsively he turned back to little Eve Edgarton's scowling face.

"Nevertheless, Miss Eve," he grinned, "I should be perfectly delighted to read your geology notes to you. Where are they?"

"Here," droned little Eve Edgarton, slapping listlessly at the loose pile of pages beside her.

Conscientiously Barton reached out and gathered the flimsy papers into one trim handful. "Where shall I begin?" he asked.

"It doesn't matter," murmured little Eve Edgarton.

"What?" said Barton. Nervously he began to fumble through the pages. "Isn't there any beginning?" he demanded.

"No," moped little Eve Edgarton.

"Nor any end?" he insisted. "Nor any middle?"

"N-o-o," sighed little Eve Edgarton.

Helplessly Barton plunged into the unhappy task before him. On page nine there were perhaps the fewest blots. He decided to begin there.

"Paleontologically," the first sentence smote him — "Paleontologically the periods are characterized by absence of the large marine saurians, Dinosaurs and Pterosaurs —"

"Eh?" gasped Barton.

"Why, of course!" called Edgarton, a bit impatiently, from the window.

Laboriously Barton went back and reread the phrase to himself. "Oh — oh, yes," he conceded lamely.

"Paleontologically," he began all over again. "Oh, dear, no!" he interrupted himself. "I was farther along than that! — Absence of marine saurians? Oh, yes!

"Absence of marine saurians," he resumed glibly, "Dinosaurs

and Pterosaurs — so abundant in the — in the Cretaceous — of Ammonites and Belemnites," he persisted — heroically. Hesitatingly, stumblingly, without a glimmer of understanding, his bewildered mind worried on and on, its entire mental energy concentrated on the single purpose of trying to pronounce the awful words.

"Of Rudistes, Inocerami — Tri — Trigonias," the horrible paragraph tortured on . . .

"By the marked reduction in the — Brachiopods compared with the now richly developed Gasteropods and — and sinupalliate — Lamellibranchs," — it writhed and twisted before his dizzy eyes.

Every sentence was a struggle; more than one of the words he was forced to spell aloud just out of sheer self-defense; and always against Eve Edgarton's little intermittent nod of encouragement was balanced that hateful sniffing sound of surprise and contempt from the orchid table in the window.

Despairingly he skipped a few lines to the next unfamiliar words that met his eye.

"The Neozoic flora," he read, "consists mainly of — of Angio — Angiosper —"

Still smiling, but distinctly wan around the edges of the smile, he slammed the handful of papers down on his knee. "If it really doesn't make any difference where we begin, Miss Eve," he said, "for Heaven's sake — let's begin somewhere else!"

"Oh — all right," crooned little Eve Edgarton.

Expeditiously Barton turned to another page, and another, and another. Wryly he tasted strange sentence after strange sentence. Then suddenly his whole wonderful face wreathed itself in smiles again.

"Three superfamilies of turtles," he began joyously. "Turtles! Ha! — I know turtles!" he proceeded with real triumph. "Why, that's the first word I've recognized in all this — this — er — this what I've been reading! Sure I know turtles!" he reiterated with increasing conviction. "Why, sure! Those — those slow-crawling, boxlike affairs that — live in the mud and are used for soup and — er — combs," he continued blithely.

"The — very — same," nodded little Eve Edgarton soberly.

"Oh — Lordy!" groaned her father from the window.

"Oh, this is going to be lots better!" beamed Barton. "Now that I know what it's all about —"

"For goodness' sake," growled Edgarton from his table, "how do you people think I'm going to do any work with all this jabbering going on!"

Hesitatingly for a moment Barton glanced back over his shoulder at Edgarton, and then turned round again to probe Eve's preferences in the matter. As sluggishly determinate as two black turtles trailing along a white sand beach, her great dark eyes in her little pale face seemed headed suddenly toward some Far-Away Idea.

"Oh — go right on reading, Mr. Barton," nodded little Eve Edgarton.

"Three superfamilies of turtles," began Barton all over again.

"Three superfamilies of turtles — the — the Amphichelydia, the Cryptodira, and the Tri — the — Tri — the T-r-i-o-n-y-c-h-o-i-d-e-a," he spelled out laboriously.

With a vicious jerk of his chair Edgarton snatched up his papers and his orchids and started for the door.

"When you people get all through this nonsense," he announced, "maybe you'll be kind enough to let me know! I shall be in the writing-room!" With satirical courtesy he bowed first to Eve, then to Barton, dallied an instant on the threshold to repeat both bows, and went out, slamming the door behind him.

"A nervous man, isn't he?" suggested Barton.

Gravely little Eve Edgarton considered the thought. "Trionychoidea," she prompted quite irrelevantly.

"Oh, yes — of course," conceded Barton. "But do you mind if I smoke?"

"No, I don't mind if you smoke," singsonged the girl.

With a palpable sigh of relief Barton lighted a cigarette. "You're nice," he said. "I like you!" Conscientiously then he resumed his reading.

"No — Pleurodira — have yet been found," he began.

"Yes — isn't that too bad?" sighed little Eve Edgarton.

"It doesn't matter personally to me," admitted Barton. Hastily he moved on to the next sentence.

"The Amphichelydia — are known there by only the genus Baena," he read.

"Two described species: B. undata and B. arenosa, to which was added B. hebraica and B. ponderosa —"

Petulantly he slammed the whole handful of papers to the floor.

"Eve!" he stammered. "I can't stand it! I tell you — I just can't stand it! Take my attic if you want to! Or my cellar! Or my garage! Or anything else of mine in the world that you have any fancy for! But for Heaven's sake —"

With extraordinarily dilated eyes Eve Edgarton stared out at him from her white pillows.

"Why — why, if it makes you feel like that — just to read it," she reproached him mournfully, "how do you suppose it makes me feel to have to write it? All you have to do — is to read it," she said. "But I? I have to write it!"

"But — why do you have to write it?" gasped Barton.

Languidly her heavy lashes shadowed down across her cheeks again. "It's for the British consul at Nunko-Nono," she said. "It's some notes he asked me to make for him in London this last spring."

"But for mercy's sake — do you like to write things like that?" insisted Barton.

"Oh, no," drawled little Eve Edgarton. "But of course — if I marry him," she confided without the slightest flicker of emotion, "it's what I'll have to write — all the rest of my life."

"But —" stammered Barton. "For mercy's sake, do you want to marry him?" he asked quite bluntly.

"Oh, no," drawled little Eve Edgarton.

Impatiently Barton threw away his half-smoked cigarette and lighted a fresh one. "Then why?" he demanded.

"Oh, it's something Father invented," said little Eve Edgarton.

Altogether emphatically Barton pushed back his chair. "Well, I call it a shame!" he said. "For a nice live little girl like you to be packed off like so much baggage — to marry some great gray-bearded clout who hasn't got an idea in his head except — except —" squintingly he stared down at the scattered sheets on the floor — "except — 'Amphichelydia,'" he asserted with some feeling.

"Yes — isn't it?" sighed little Eve Edgarton.

"For Heaven's sake!" said Barton. "Where is Nunko-Nono?"

"Nunko-Nono?" whispered little Eve Edgarton. "Where is it? Why, it's an island! In an ocean, you know! Rather a hot — green island! In rather a hot — blue-green ocean! Lots of green palms, you know, and rank, rough, green grass — and green bugs — and green butterflies — and green snakes. And a great crawling, crunching collar of white sand and hermit-crabs all around it. And then just a long, unbroken line of turquoise-colored waves. And then more turquoise-colored waves. And then more turquoise-colored waves. And then more turquoise-colored waves. And then — and then —"

"And then what?" worried Barton.

With a vaguely astonished lift of the eyebrows little Eve Edgarton met both question and questioner perfectly squarely. "Why — then — more turquoise-colored waves, of course," chanted little Eve Edgarton.

"It sounds rotten to me," confided Barton.

"It is," said little Eve Edgarton. "And, oh, I forgot to tell you: John Ellbertson is — sort of green, too. Geologists are apt to be, don't you think so?"

"I never saw one," admitted Barton without shame.

"If you'd like me to," said Eve, "I'll show you how the turquoise-colored waves sound — when they strike the hermit-crabs."

"Do!" urged Barton.

Listlessly the girl pushed back into her pillows, slid down a little farther into her blankets, and closed her eyes.

"Mmmmmmmmmm," she began, "Mmmmmmmmmmm — Mmmmm — Mmmmmmmm, W-h-i-s-h-h-h! Mmmmmmmmm — Mmmmmm — Mmmmmm — Mmmmmm — W-h-i-s-h-h-h! — Mmmmmm — Mmmmmmm —"

"After a while, of course, I think you might stop," suggested Barton a bit creepishly.

Again the big eyes opened at him with distinct surprise. "Why — why?" said Eve Edgarton. "It — never stops!"

"Oh, I say," frowned Barton, "I do feel awfully badly about your going away off to a place like that to live! Really!" he stammered.

"We're going — Thursday," said little Eve Edgarton.

"*Thursday?*" cried Barton. For some inexplainable reason the whole idea struck him suddenly as offensive, distinctly offensive, as if Fate, the impatient waiter, had snatched away a yet untasted plate. "Why — why, Eve!" he protested, "why, we're only just beginning to get acquainted."

"Yes, I know it," mused little Eve Edgarton.

"Why — if we'd have had half a chance —" began Barton, and then didn't know at all how to finish it. "Why, you're so plucky — and so odd — and so interesting!" he began all over again. "Oh, of course, I'm an awful duffer and all that! But if we'd had half a chance, I say, you and I would have been great pals in another fortnight!"

"Even so," murmured little Eve Edgarton, "there are yet — fifty-two hours before I go."

"What are fifty-two hours?" laughed Barton.

Listlessly like a wilting flower little Eve Edgarton slid down a trifle farther into her pillows. "If you'd have an early supper," she whispered, "and then come right up here afterward, why, there would be two or three hours. And then tomorrow if you got up quite early, there would be a long, long morning, and — we — could get acquainted — some," she insisted.

"Why, Eve!" said Barton, "do you really mean that you would like to be friends with me?"

"Yes — I do," nodded the crown of the white-bandaged head.

"But I'm so stupid," confided Barton, with astonishing humility. "All these botany things — and geology — and —"

"Yes, I know it," mumbled little Eve Edgarton. "That's what makes you so restful."

"What?" queried Barton a bit sharply. Then very absent-mindedly for a moment he sat staring off into space through a gray, pungent haze of cigarette smoke.

"Eve," he ventured at last.

"What?" mumbled little Eve Edgarton.

"Nothing," said Barton.

"Mr. Jim Barton," ventured Eve.

"What?" asked Barton.

"Nothing," mumbled little Eve Edgarton.

Out of some emotional or purely social tensities of life it seems rather that Time strikes the clock than that anything so small as a clock should dare strike the Time. One — two — three — four — five! winced the poor little frightened traveling-clock on the mantelpiece.

Then quite abruptly little Eve Edgarton emerged from her cozy cushions, sitting bolt upright like a doughty little warrior.

"Mr. Jim Barton!" said little Eve Edgarton. "If I stayed here two weeks longer — I know you'd like me! I know it! I just know it!" Quizzically for an instant, as if to accumulate further courage, she cocked her little head on one side and stared blankly into Barton's astonished eyes. "But you see I'm not going to be here two weeks!" she resumed hurriedly. Again the little head cocked appealingly to one side. "You — you wouldn't be willing to take my word for it, would you? And like me — now?"

"Why — why, what do you mean?" stammered Barton.

"What do I mean?" quizzed little Eve Edgarton. "Why, I mean — that just once before I go off to Nunko-Nono — I'd like to be — attractive!"

"Attractive?" stammered Barton helplessly.

With all the desperate, indomitable frankness of a child, the girl's chin thrust itself forward.

"I could be attractive!" she said. "I could! I know I could! If I'd ever let go just the teeniest — tiniest bit — I could have — beaux!" she asserted triumphantly. "A thousand beaux!" she added more explicitly. "Only —"

"Only what?" laughed Barton.

"Only one doesn't let go," said little Eve Edgarton.

"Why not?" persisted Barton.

"Why, you just — couldn't — with strangers," said little Eve Edgarton. "That's the bewitchment of it."

"The bewitchment?" puzzled Barton.

Nervously the girl crossed her hands in her lap. She suddenly didn't look like a doughty little soldier any more, but just like a worried little girl.

"Did you ever read any fairy stories?" she asked with apparent irrelevance.

"Why, of course," said Barton. "Millions of them when I was a kid."

"I read one — once," said little Eve Edgarton. "It was about a person, a sleeping person, a lady, I mean, who couldn't wake up until a prince kissed her. Well, that was all right, of course," conceded little Eve Edgarton, "because, of course, any prince would have been willing to kiss the lady just as a mere matter of accommodation. But suppose," fretted little Eve Edgarton, "suppose the bewitchment also ran that no prince would kiss the lady until she had waked up? Now there!" said little Eve Edgarton, "is a situation that I should call completely stalled."

"But what's all this got to do with you?" grinned Barton.

"Nothing at all to do with me!" said little Eve Edgarton. "It is me! That's just exactly the way I'm fixed. I can't be attractive — out loud — until some one likes me! But no one, of course, will ever like me until I am already attractive — out loud! So that's why I wondered," she said, "if just as a mere matter of accommodation, you wouldn't be willing to be friends with me now? So that for at least the fifty-two hours that remain, I could be released — from my most unhappy enchantment."

Astonishingly across that frank, perfectly outspoken little face, the frightened eyelashes came flickering suddenly down. "Because," whispered little Eve Edgarton, "because — you see — I happen to like you already."

"Oh, fine!" smiled Barton. "Fine! Fine! Fi —" Abruptly the word broke in his throat. "What?" he cried. His hand — the steadiest hand among all his chums — began to shake like an aspen. "*What?*" he cried. His heart, the steadiest heart among all his chums, began to pitch and lurch in his breast. "Why, Eve! Eve!" he stammered. "You don't mean you like me — like that?"

"Yes — I do," nodded the little white-capped head. There was much shyness of flesh in the statement, but not a flicker of spiritual self-consciousness or fear.

"But — Eve!" protested Barton. Already he felt the gooseflesh rising on his arms. Once before a girl had told him that she — liked him. In the middle of a silly summer flirtation it had been, and the scene had been mawkish, awful, a mess of tears and kisses and endless recriminations. But this girl? Before the utter simplicity of this girl's statement, the unruffled dignity, the mere acknowledgment, as it were, of an interesting historical fact, all his trifling, preconceived ideas went tumbling down before his eyes like a flimsy house of cards. Pang after pang of regret for the girl, of regret for himself, went surging hotly through him. "Oh, but — Eve!" he began all over again. His voice was raw with misery.

"Why, there's nothing to make a fuss about," drawled little Eve Edgarton. "You've probably liked a thousand people, but I — you see? — I've never had the fun of liking — any one — before!"

"Fun?" tortured Barton. "Yes, that's just it! If you'd ever had the fun of liking anything it wouldn't seem half so brutal — now!"

"Brutal?" mused little Eve Edgarton. "Oh, really, Mr. Jim Barton, I assure you," she said, "there's nothing brutal at all in my liking — for you."

With a gasp of despair Barton stumbled across the rug to the bed, and with a shaky hand thrust under Eve Edgarton's chin, turned her little face bluntly up to him to tell her — how proud he felt, but — to tell her how sorry he was, but —

And as he turned that little face up to his, — inconceivably — incomprehensively — to his utter consternation and rout — he saw that it was a stranger's little face that he held. Gone was the sullen frown, the indifferent glance, the bitter smile, and in that sudden, amazing, wild, sweet transfiguration of brow, eyes, mouth, that met his astonished eyes, he felt his whole mean, supercilious world slip out from under his feet! And just as precipitously, just as inexplainably, as ten days before he had seen a Great Light that had knocked all consciousness out of him, he experienced now a second Great Light that knocked him back into the first full consciousness that he had ever known!

"Why, Eve!" he stammered. "Why, you — mischief! Why, you little — cheeky darling! Why, my own — darned little Story Book Girl!" And gathered her into his arms.

From the farther side of the room the sound of a creaking board smote almost instantly upon their ears.

"Any time that you people want me," suggested Edgarton's icy voice, "I am standing here — in about the middle of the floor!"

With a jerk of dismay Barton wheeled around to face him. But it was little Eve Edgarton herself who found her tongue first.

"Oh, Father dear — I have been perfectly wise!" she hastened to assure him. "Almost at once, Father, I told him that I liked him, so that if he really were the dreadful kind of young man you were warning me about, he would eliminate himself from my horizon — immediately — in his wicked pursuit of — some other lady!

Oh, he did run, Father!" she confessed in the first red blush of her life. "Oh, he did — run, Father, but it was — almost directly — toward me!"

"Eh?" snapped Edgarton.

Then in a divine effrontery, half impudence and half humility, Barton stepped out into the middle of the room, and proffered his strong, firm young hand to the older man.

"You told me," he grinned, "to rummage around until I discovered a Real Treasure? Well, I didn't have to do it! It was the Treasure, it seems, who discovered me!"

Then suddenly into his fine young eyes flared up the first glint of his newborn soul.

"Your daughter, sir," said Barton, "is the most beautiful woman in the world! As you suggested to me, I have found out what she is interested in — She is interested in — *me!*"